"She wakes up at night crying."

Johnny spoke as if the image his words conjured pained him. He turned to her then, more serious than she'd ever seen him. "I realize we won't have one of those one-in-a-million kind of marriages, Grace, but we've got friendship going for us, haven't we?"

His blue eyes were intent, warming her clear to that place in her heart that had always been just for him. She recognized the yearning inside her, just as she saw quite clearly that Johnny knew no such feeling, that because of his parents, he had no true concept of what love was.

He reached out and tentatively covered her hand with his. "I know it's asking a lot. But I'm asking for Gracie's sake. Will you marry me?"

Hadn't she seen right away that Johnny would do anything for Gracie?

Even marry her.

And Grace said softly, "Yes."

Dear Reader,

Traditionally June is the month for weddings, so Silhouette Romance cordially invites you to enjoy our promotion JUNE BRIDES, starting with Suzanne Carey's *Sweet Bride of Revenge.* In this sensuously powerful VIRGIN BRIDES tale, a man forces the daughter of his nemesis to marry him, never counting on falling in love with the enemy....

Up-and-comer Robin Nicholas delivers a touching BUNDLES OF JOY titled *Man, Wife and Little Wonder.* Can a denim-clad, Harley-riding bad boy turn doting dad and dedicated husband? Find out in this classic marriage-of-convenience romance! Next, Donna Clayton's delightful duo MOTHER & CHILD continues with the evocative title *Who's the Father of Jenny's Baby?* A woman awakens in the hospital to discover she has amnesia—and she's pregnant! Problem is, *two* men claim to be the baby's father—her estranged husband...and her husband's brother!

Granted: Wild West Bride is the next installment in Carol Grace's BEST-KEPT WISHES series. This richly Western romance pairs a toughened, taut-muscled cowboy and a sophisticated city gal who welcomes his kisses, but will she accept his ring? For a fresh spin on the bridal theme, try Alice Sharpe's *Wife on His Doorstep.* An about-to-be bride stops her wedding to the wrong man, only to land on the doorstep of the strong, silent ship captain who was to perform the ill-fated nuptials.... And in Leanna Wilson's latest Romance, *His Tomboy Bride,* Nick Latham was *supposed* to "give away" childhood friend and bride-to-be Billie Rae—not claim the transformed beauty as his own!

We hope you enjoy the month's wedding fun, and return each and every month for more classic, emotional, heartwarming novels from Silhouette Romance.

Enjoy!

Joan Marlow Golan

Joan Marlow Golan
Senior Editor Silhouette Romance

Please address questions and book requests to:
Silhouette Reader Service
U.S.: 3010 Walden Ave., P.O. Box 1325, Buffalo, NY 14269
Canadian: P.O. Box 609, Fort Erie, Ont. L2A 5X3

MAN, WIFE AND LITTLE WONDER

Robin Nicholas

Silhouette
R O M A N C E™
Published by Silhouette Books
America's Publisher of Contemporary Romance

To Marilyn Sue Lemmon for her generous support of my career, and for giving me the kind of encouragement only another writer can give.

SPECIAL THANKS
To attorney-at-law and fellow author Lauren Phelps for her help with the legal technicalities.

 SILHOUETTE BOOKS

ISBN 0-373-19301-7

MAN, WIFE AND LITTLE WONDER

Copyright © 1998 by Robin Kapala

Printed in U.S.A.

Books by Robin Nicholas

Silhouette Romance

The Cowboy and His Lady #1017
Wrangler's Wedding #1049
Man, Wife and Little Wonder #1301

ROBIN NICHOLAS

lives in Illinois with her husband, Dan, and their son, Nick. Her debut book, *The Cowboy and His Lady*, was part of the successful Silhouette Romance CELEBRATION 1000 promotion. Her current BUNDLES OF JOY feature is her third book for the line, and her fourth Romance novel will be available in the fall of 1998.

Bundles of JOY

Dear Reader,

Having a book chosen for the BUNDLES OF JOY
promotion is a very special occasion for me. My son,
Nick, is certainly the greatest joy of my life. Through
Nick and his cousins, Beth, Kris, Katie, Kyle, Nicholee
and Garrett, Shandee and Micah, Justin and Lauren, I
have found a constant source of pride, inspiration,
laughter and love.

BUNDLES OF JOY celebrates the belief that the
wonder of a child can bring to light the love between a
man and a woman. I invite you to celebrate that belief
with me, as well, in the story of Johnny, Grace and little
Gracie in *Man, Wife and Little Wonder.*

I hope you enjoy the book.

Sincerely,

Robin Nicholas

Chapter One

He was back.

Grace Marie Green tightened her grip on the open door to the Grace Marie Salon. A hot August breeze fanned her face while ribbons of heat rose from the glossy black and silver motorcycle parked diagonally at the curb. Straddling the bike, looking much like the teenage boy she'd once secretly worshiped, was Johnny Tremont.

Johnny pulled off dark glasses and took in his surroundings. Grace caught the gleam in his blue eyes as he removed his helmet, freeing his thick black hair. He stared straight into her green eyes, seeming to absorb all the changes of the past ten years in a matter of seconds. Then, flashing the smile that had once convinced her to let him siphon gas for his Harley from her daddy's John Deere, he said, "Gracie needs a haircut. And I need you to marry me."

The noonday heat hit her full in the face and Grace braced herself with a hand on the door frame. She felt almost faint. And she thought she'd just heard Johnny say he needed her to marry him. It had to be this hot weather, causing some kind of hallucination....

Her heart caught as a small body leaned from behind Johnny's back, a child clad in pink T-shirt and jeans and wearing a pink and black helmet that probably cost more than a year's worth of spiral perms. Johnny lifted the helmet from the child's head, revealing dark hair and blue eyes. She knew without a doubt that this pretty child of four was Johnny's niece, and her namesake, little Gracie.

"Is now okay?"

Johnny's innocent voice drifted over her, as the sun slanted down, casting a deceptive halo over his gleaming black hair. Grace drew a deep breath. Johnny had said Gracie needed a haircut. She had only imagined the rest. Though it was Monday and the salon was officially closed, she said automatically, "Now is fine."

"We can talk about getting married afterward," Johnny said.

That feeling of faintness assailed Grace again.

It hadn't been a hallucination....

Johnny dismounted and lifted Gracie, carrying the child past her, making brief but potent contact as his arms and legs and hips touched hers, his breath whisking her bangs across her forehead. Grace thought how little her life had changed over the years. But as Johnny brushed by, she could sense a change in the air.

Grace shut the door. *What was going on here?* Why had Johnny, who had always seen her as a pesky second sister, said such a thing? Hearing the words she'd once dreamed of hearing as an awkward teen only made her angry with him now.

Gracie observed her from where Johnny settled the child on her feet, and Grace's heart softened. *Too solemn,* Grace thought, and as the little girl glanced away, *too shy.* Johnny's sister, Janelle, had been shy, and Grace felt the same protective instinct for Gracie that she'd felt for her best friend. The feeling was compounded by the accidental death of Gracie's parents one month earlier, which she assumed had left the child under the guardianship of her maternal grandparents. Too distraught to make the three-hour drive to Chicago, Grace hadn't attended the funeral. She tried, but failed, to imagine Gracie being raised by the highbrow Tremonts.

Conscious of Johnny's watchful gaze, Grace stepped into the room, a wariness coming over her that she recognized from years ago whenever Johnny would try to draw her and Janelle into one of his pranks.

I need you to marry me.

Johnny had been smiling as he spoke and Grace realized he'd been teasing. He'd probably gotten a charge out of the shock value of his words. She'd fallen for his joke, of course, just the way she used to.

Most likely, Johnny had brought his niece from Chicago to the country to see where her mother once lived.

Johnny leaned down and whispered in Gracie's ear. Then Gracie ran over to one of the styling stations and climbed into a chair. With her hand, she pushed off from the counter to set the chair twirling and creaking. Her hair, damp with sweat from the helmet, hung limply to her shoulders and clung to her head.

Grace planted her hands on her hips, frowning at Johnny. "That little girl has no business riding on a motorcycle."

Though he'd taken a lazy stance, Johnny's lean body seemed to simmer. His once shaggy hair was now cut in a stylish wedge, short on the sides, long on top. His T-shirt was plain white, devoid of snakes, chains or four-letter words. He wore jeans that looked soft, faded by design rather than as a show of rebellion, and a pair of pricey white high-top tennis shoes, which replaced the leather boots he used to favor. To the average eye, Johnny appeared to have changed.

But Grace had never seen Johnny in the same light as any average person, and with just a glance, she knew better. Johnny Tremont hadn't changed.

"We only drove from the motel at the edge of town." His nonchalant tone failed to reassure her. "A friend hauled us and the Harley down from Chicago last night."

"So you could marry me." Grace laced her voice

with sarcasm, letting him know he hadn't fooled her with his "proposal." She was twenty-five, not fifteen. She didn't have stars in her eyes anymore.

But her sarcasm bounced right off Johnny.

"That's right." There was purpose in his step as he drew closer, resolve in his voice as he lowered it to tell her, "In their will, Janelle and Grant named me Gracie's legal guardian. Now Mother and Dad are suing for guardianship on the grounds that I'm unfit to raise her. I intend to keep Gracie, but to do that, I need a wife. I need you to marry me."

Johnny's words hadn't lost any of their shock value with repetition. On an indrawn breath she whispered a sentiment once shared by all of Ashville, Illinois. "You're crazy, Johnny."

"I've never been more sane—or serious—in my life," he responded without hesitation, his jaw set, his eyes more grave than she'd ever seen them.

Johnny, a father figure? The idea defied imagination. But apparently he'd served as one since Janelle and Grant's deaths.

"Mother's playing the part to impress her friends. Dad's indulging her." His voice grew bitter. "They don't really want Gracie."

Grace recalled how the wealthy Tremonts had originally bought the acreage outside of town, near the Green farm, with the hope that quiet country life would keep fifteen-year-old Johnny out of trouble and coax Janelle out of shyness. But their busy lives hadn't allowed them time for Johnny and Janelle. They'd paid for Johnny's pranks and had been relieved when Janelle found a friend to keep her amused.

She realized Johnny was right. The Tremonts had never seemed to want Johnny and Janelle. Why would they want Gracie?

"I want to raise Gracie here in Ashville," Johnny went on. "But the court won't allow it unless I can provide a better life for her than my parents."

"That doesn't necessarily mean you have to marry," she insisted, her sense of self-preservation kicking in full tilt.

"According to my lawyer, it does." Johnny's reply was grim. Marriage had not likely been his first solution to his problem. But it was evident he meant to follow through on his lawyer's advice, that he meant to marry *her*.

"I realize I'm asking a lot. But I intend to make this worth your while by paying off the mortgage on your farm, whatever the outcome in court."

Heat burned Grace's cheeks. He was *paying* her to marry him. Nothing could have made it more clear—he still saw her as something less than a desirable woman.

"Once I have guardianship of Gracie, and Mother gets back to her tea parties, we can divorce."

Nothing except that.

Grace felt a flare of indignation. Worse, she felt all of fifteen again, desperate for Johnny to see her as a woman. *A woman in love with him...*

Her heart missed a panicked beat. She couldn't do this.

She was about to tell Johnny so when his gaze cut to Gracie, and she saw a fierce protectiveness come into his eyes, tinged with a trace of desperation. She caught her lip. Johnny, who had never needed anything but his motorcycles and the successful dealership and repair shop he'd started in Chicago, needed her help with Gracie.

Suddenly aware of the quiet, she realized the chair had stopped creaking and Gracie sat watching them, her eyes revealing the sadness inside her.

A sense of fate rolled over Grace. But she only whispered to Johnny, "I don't know. I need time to think."

But she couldn't think clearly standing so close to Johnny. She walked over to the styling station and summoned a smile for Gracie. She pumped the chair as high as it would go, rewarded when Gracie's lips curved and the little girl leaned to watch the floor descend. She didn't use the booster chair, because she wanted Gracie to feel like a big girl.

"Just, uh, cut a little off the bottom…" Johnny's voice trailed off at her baleful stare.

Grace spun Gracie to face the mirror. "How would *you* like your hair cut, Gracie?"

Gracie stared at her pink tennis shoes. Johnny shifted, and this time Grace warned him clearly with her gaze to keep quiet.

"Like yours," Gracie finally said.

"Excellent choice." Grace smiled, her heart turning over. No one had ever wanted to look like her before.

She set to work, tying a pink plastic apron beneath Gracie's chin. Aware of Johnny's close regard, she wondered if he noticed that her once long brown hair now swung neatly at her shoulders, that she wore a touch of makeup and a fashionable denim jumper over her crisp white T-shirt. She thought of the ill-fitting clothes and unstyled hair she'd had in high school. She hadn't exactly been prom material.

But then, in his own way, neither had Johnny.

She parted Gracie's silky hair while Johnny circled the room, skirting hair care displays and the potted plants she'd been watering. His straight nose wrinkled over the lingering scents of solutions and shampoos. He eyed the photos on the wall of models with elaborate hairdos, coming to a halt before the cash register. Behind it, she'd hung a picture of Elvis sporting a ducktail, in deference to the retro look.

"I remember that picture," he said.

Of course he remembered. Her parents had been Elvis fans, in their thirties during Elvis's heyday of movies and songs, when they'd fallen in love. The front hall of the old farmhouse where Grace had lived since her parents' deaths had been decorated with photos of Elvis when she and Janelle and Johnny were teens. The one time she'd danced with Johnny had been in the living room to a slow Elvis tune.

"Can't Help Falling In Love."

Grace shook off the wistful feeling that came over her and gazed at Johnny with a critical eye. He was handsome with his hair cut in that crisp wedge, falling sexily over his forehead. With a ducktail he would look like a devastatingly young Elvis.

He turned then and caught her staring. Hiding her attraction, the way she'd always done, she said haughtily, "A shampoo and trim would do wonders for you."

Johnny's gaze glinted right back at her. "I have a *barber* in the city. And he doesn't give *shampoos*."

Grace turned away to hide her grin. She'd missed the exhilarating rush that came with sparring with Johnny. She'd missed *Johnny*. Before she could stop the thought, Grace imagined, as she had long ago, what it would be like if he really wanted to marry her.

But he'd come back for Gracie's sake.

They needed to talk and so she hurried little Gracie's trim along. Grace was aware from the way Johnny jingled his keys in his pocket that his patience was running out.

Johnny managed not to reach up and push his hand through his hair. He was due for a trip to the barber but he'd be damned if he'd sit in that chair with a pink bib tied around his neck.

Gracie seemed to enjoy getting her hair cut, though. And her smile cut right through to Johnny's heart. He knew the pain that lurked beneath the surface, knew how Gracie cried in the night, how she clung to him if he had to leave her for a short while, afraid that, like her parents, he wouldn't come back.

Johnny didn't leave Gracie anymore. He ran his

business by phone. He'd stopped partying, stopped *everything* for Gracie. He'd turned his world upside down to make her happy. He wasn't going to lose her now to *his* parents.

Which meant, according to his lawyer, that he had to clean up his act. Provide a loving home life to rival that of his respectable, wealthy parents.

What a joke.

Gracie wasn't going to grow up in the same cold environment he and Janelle had. Not if he could help it. Not if Grace would marry him.

Frowning, Johnny contemplated Grace. She and Janelle had exchanged occasional letters. Through Janelle he'd learned that Grace was hanging on to that farm by a thread, and that there was no special man in her life. Maybe his proposal was a little sudden, but he could see that she wanted to help Gracie. He couldn't understand what held her back.

But then, Grace had always been independent. Though she'd never let him down, she'd never been as easily swayed as Janelle to help him in and out of mischief.

He trailed his gaze the length of Grace's body, over the soft curves that rounded the angles she'd had as a teen. Grace had almost seemed like a sister to him back then, but now...

Snipping little Gracie's bangs expertly with scissors, Grace caught his gaze. "What?"

"I'd pictured you married by now," he lied, a little shocked to think he'd imagined that slip of a dress falling to her ankles.

"I pictured you married by now to a bleached blonde wearing spandex." Grace pursed her lips against a smile. "Spandex over silicone."

He laughed. A spark of fun had always lurked within Grace even though her life, which had revolved around her mother's Alzheimer's disease and resulting financial struggles, had forced her to be responsible and serious. It occurred to Johnny that she didn't deserve to wind up married to someone like him, even for a little while. She deserved a happily-ever-after kind of guy, one who believed in the game of hearts and flowers and rings. One who believed in love.

But she was just the kind of girl he needed to marry, with her wholesome country upbringing. And he knew she would be good for Gracie, the way she'd been good for shy Janelle.

Grace leaned to snip Gracie's bangs, her dress hugging her curves—a woman's curves. Johnny narrowed his gaze. Grace might have acquired a boyfriend in the past month. She might already be engaged to some other guy. He scanned her busy fingers for a ring, but she was moving this way and that, clipping Gracie's hair, and he couldn't see. He shifted impatiently.

Gracie, meanwhile, sat like a queen, her little chin lifted in clear imitation of Grace. He was counting on Grace to draw Gracie out of her shell, the way she had Janelle. But he hadn't expected the effect of Grace's personality to rub off so quickly. He was more certain than ever that Grace would be good for

Gracie, and that he'd done the right thing in coming here.

Grace sensed Johnny's scrutiny, his impatience. She gave little Gracie's hair a final combing, then smiled. "In the drawer by the cash register, there's a box of ribbons and barrettes. You can go pick out some if you'd like."

Gracie gave a quick nod and climbed from the chair, hurrying over to open the drawer. Grace watched her, while a keen awareness of Johnny's slow approach radiated through her.

"We need to talk," he said, echoing her earlier thought in a low voice. He stood close, and she caught the scent of him, still with that hint of motor oil. His belly was flat as it had been when he left town at eighteen, and he looked solid and strong in his white T-shirt. His gaze was unwavering, and it was hard to believe Johnny needed her for anything.

Then the light in his eyes changed, and her heartbeat changed with it. That dark promise she read in Johnny's gaze was not the kind of promise a brother made to a sister.

But before she could be sure of it, before she could take it to heart, Gracie ran over to them, diverting Johnny. Holding a pink ribbon in each hand, she told him, "I'm hungry."

Johnny gave Grace a beguiling smile and, as if they were already married, asked, "What's for lunch?"

With a brief glare for Johnny, Grace smoothed little Gracie's hair. "How would you like to have lunch on a farm, Gracie?"

"Is there a cow?"

She couldn't help but laugh. "No cow. But there are kittens you can play with and flowers you can pick."

Gracie's smile was Janelle's smile. It was both endearing and heartbreaking. Grace turned away, but there was no escaping her sorrow, a sorrow that didn't begin to compare to Gracie's. Grabbing a can of styling spray, she said quickly, "First, let's fix those ribbons in your hair."

Gracie looked longingly at the pink can of spray, the kind her mom used to buy. "Can I, Johnny?"

No "uncle," just Johnny, Grace noted. Leave it to Johnny to waive the formalities.

He gave his consent in the form of a wary shrug, standing well away from the spray while Grace lightly misted Gracie's hair. Minutes later, they exited the shop.

Little Gracie was adorable and Grace felt a pride in Janelle's child, a pride she supposed Janelle had felt tenfold. She imagined herself brushing Gracie's hair each morning, tucking her into bed at night.

She imagined tucking Johnny into bed, too....

"Hey, Gold Groceries is still open?" Johnny said, pointing just down the street at the store's sign.

Grace always thought it had been Johnny who'd thrown the rock that broke the bulb that lit up the "G," leaving the sign to read "old" Groceries.

"Let's walk down there and I'll get some stuff for lunch."

She glanced uneasily at Johnny. "I have plenty of food at the farm."

"Bet you don't have the right kind of peanut butter. Come on, I want Gracie to see Gold's. I remember hanging around there, drinking pop and watching girls."

"I remember you were banned from the store," Grace muttered, hoping by *get* some stuff for lunch, Johnny meant he would pay for it. His parents had paid dearly for the fireworks he'd stolen.

Grace started after him, certain Henry Gold wouldn't share Johnny's enthusiasm if he knew Johnny was coming to his store.

As they walked down the street, Gracie skipped before them, never more than two cracks in the sidewalk ahead. Grace thought all of Ashville must be watching and wondering over Johnny's return. She imagined the last thing they would think was that he'd come back to marry her.

Although, watching Gracie's carefree skipping, Grace could understand Johnny's desire to raise his shy niece in the quiet town of Ashville as opposed to the city. She pressed her lips wryly. She could understand, as well, why Johnny's lawyer thought marriage would make the court more amenable to his keeping guardianship of Gracie.

Johnny drifted closer to her side, until his arm brushed her shoulder and their hips met occasionally, the skirt of her jumper ruffled by the brush of his jeans. She wanted to look up at him, see the blue-black shine of his hair in the sun, but she ignored the impulse. Instead, she contemplated the prospect of Johnny raising Gracie, when all he'd ever raised was Cain.

She wanted to help Gracie, too. But the truth was, she didn't know much more about kids than Johnny. Her mother's struggle with Alzheimer's had resulted in her spending many hours at home or at the Ashville Nursing Home, instead of baby-sitting like most teenage girls. And the idea of marriage to Johnny, once a dream of hers, seemed only a painful prospect, with the knowledge that he didn't love her.

Gracie spotted the store, interrupting Grace's thoughts with her excitement as she read her initial, *G*, on the sign to Johnny.

Johnny grinned. "Just seeing that place makes me want a beefstick and a cola."

"Hardly an appropriate lunch for a little girl," Grace pointed out, certain that was just what he had in mind.

"I like peanut butter," Gracie said.

"With celery," Johnny added. "Let's go."

Inside, the store was cool and dim and quiet. Henry came from behind the counter, wearing a clean white apron over his bib overalls. His frown had left wrinkles over the years, and his drawn eyebrows were now white, matching the wispy hair on his head. Johnny towered over him at six feet, but that didn't keep Henry from aiming his famous glare at Johnny.

"Well, if it ain't Johnny Tremont. Heard you was in jail and heard you was rich. Which is it?"

"Well, I'm not in jail," Johnny said pointedly, leaving Grace to hope he would mind his temper.

"Humph. I got mirrors now." Henry pointed his gnarled finger over the door and to a back corner of the little square store. "And alarms." Henry nodded toward Gracie. "Who have you got there?"

Grace expected little Gracie to wilt beneath Henry's perpetual glare. But Gracie only stared at Henry, a funny little smile on her face.

Johnny rested his hand on Gracie's shoulder. "This is my niece, Gracie."

As much as was possible, Henry's face softened. "I was sorry to hear about Janelle." Then he added meaningfully, "She was a good girl." He frowned down at Gracie. "Are you a good girl?"

Gracie nodded vigorously. "Johnny said so."

"Humph. Don't break anything in the store. If you don't break anything, I'll give you a candy." Henry shuffled behind the counter, mumbling about apples falling close to the tree.

Johnny drew a deep breath and headed down the aisle to the peanut butter. Grace knew he would find it in the same place that it had been ten years ago.

"He's *Grumpy,*" Gracie chimed, looking back at Henry.

"Old grouch hasn't changed any, that's for sure," Johnny muttered.

"No, like Grumpy the dwarf," Gracie explained.

Grace laughed. "You mean the dwarf in *Snow White?*"

"Johnny reads it to me," Gracie said, choosing peanut butter and leaving Grace to contend with the appealing image of Johnny reading a fairy tale, his niece cuddled beside him.

In all her years of daydreaming about Johnny, it was certainly not something she'd ever imagined before.

Gracie's presence seemed to have quite an effect on Johnny. Years ago, Johnny and Henry had had a running feud, Johnny laughing off every battle. Now he almost seemed bothered by his lingering reputation, most likely because of Gracie.

Along with Gracie's peanut butter, they chose oranges and celery and ham. Grace insisted she had anything else they might need, but when they reached the counter, Gracie wanted cupcakes. Johnny immediately went in search of the treat with Gracie, holding his niece's hand. Grace dug in her skirt pocket for quarters to buy Gracie candy, thinking maybe Johnny had changed some after all—

A crash came from the back of the store, followed by the thunder of rolling canned goods.

Grace closed her eyes. *Maybe not.*

Chapter Two

Gracie.

Grace dropped her quarters on the counter. Henry glared into the mirror over the door, that look of old in his eyes. Ignoring him, she ran to the pyramid of soup cans she'd seen at the back of the store.

She found Johnny holding Gracie safe in his arms, cans rocking to a halt at his feet.

His anxious gaze met Grace's over top of the little girl's head. His breath rushed out. "She's all right."

Grace felt the tension leave her, only to have it rise again as Henry came to survey the damage, something he'd done often in Johnny's presence. In the quiet aftermath, the whir of a ceiling fan brought to mind the time Johnny had dropped a bag of flour in front of Henry's old floor model fan. Grace caught her lip, recalling the shouting match that had ensued. Actually, it had seemed funny at the time.

Henry glowered at Johnny. "Figured it was you."

Gracie clutched her arms about Johnny's neck. "Johnny didn't do it."

"Humph. Heard that before."

Gracie's soft little arms squeezed the defiance right out of Johnny. He wasn't going to get in a yelling match with old Henry, not with Gracie listening—and Grace.

Johnny narrowed his gaze. Grace was trying not to laugh, her eyes sparkling at him. A sense of déjà vu washed over him. He recalled Grace laughing at him that way years ago, as he stood in this store, powdered with flour, Henry dusted with it, too, while the old man called him a delinquent.

And they said you couldn't go home again.

Johnny stood rooted in the past, recalling the way Grace had laughed at him that day, her long hair spilling past the shoulders of the faded shirt she wore. In some ways, she'd changed. Her hair now swung across her shoulders, which were covered in the soft white cotton of a formfitting T-shirt beneath the sassy little dress she wore. She looked sexy as hell.

But in another way, she was still the same Grace, daring to laugh at him with those green eyes.

And that was sexy, too.

"You clean this up, Johnny Tremont. I've got a customer. And don't forget, I've got mirrors." Henry turned toward the front of the store, muttering about dented cans and delinquents.

Grace grinned openly and Johnny shot her a menacing look. She'd watched him sweep up flour years ago, grinning at him over the rim of a cola bottle. "Are you going to help stack these cans, or just stand and watch?"

Gracie squirmed, wanting down. "Can I help?"

Johnny set little Gracie on her feet. "You bet. We'll rebuild the pyramid and you can put on the top can. Do you think we should *let* Grace help?"

Gracie gave a quick nod.

"You're in," Johnny said, smirking at Grace.

She was a good sport—too much so, Johnny decided. Grace crouched in her flirty dress, giving him flashes of smooth slim thigh as they worked toward the center of the pile from opposite directions. Little Gracie had a great time, while Johnny suffered.

Until the moment he saw Grace again, Johnny had only thought of marriage to her in terms of keeping guardianship of Gracie. Now he found himself rethinking the idea on a more primal level.

There were a lot of cans, and he gave Gracie a break, sending her to put the cupcakes on Henry's counter. He and Grace had inched almost nose to nose, and as their knees brushed, she wobbled. He reached out and curled his hand about her arm, and the softness of her skin stilled him.

He knew Grace felt his tension when she paused. He smoothed his thumb across her skin and got a jolt out of her direct gaze.

He wondered what she'd do if he kissed her.

Never one to wonder for long, Johnny leaned closer. Grace smelled heavenly. Sweet and womanly, a potent combination. Her eyes seemed to glaze over, focused on his mouth as he eased it toward her pink parted lips—

"Henry's got mirrors," she whispered, not quite breaking the spell. They hovered inches apart, Johnny not giving a damn about mirrors, yet aware it probably mattered to Grace, who likely remembered what a kiss with Johnny Tremont used to mean to a girl's reputation in Ashville—never mind if a kiss had been all that had happened.

Gracie came running back then and Johnny didn't miss the quick way Grace backed off. Even faster than he. He could feel her wary gaze upon him, though, likely seeing him in a new light. She'd probably always thought of him as a pesky older brother, in the same way he'd thought of her as a sister. So all these sexual vibes bouncing between them had to be as much a shock to her as they were to him.

Johnny stacked the remaining cans, lifting Gracie to place the last one on top as promised. Their task accomplished, the three of them headed for the front of the store. Johnny was aware that Grace kept her distance.

Under Henry's watchful eye, Johnny paid for his purchases. He hoisted the sack in his arms and led the way to the door.

"Come get a candy, little girl," Henry called to Gracie, amazing Johnny. Even more amazing, Gracie ran back and Henry handed a lollipop down to her.

"Thank you," Gracie said in a near whisper.

Johnny couldn't have been more surprised if Gracie had shouted. Not that Gracie was ill-mannered; she was usually just too shy to talk, without Johnny by her side to prompt the conversation. But then, Gracie thought Henry was a dwarf.

Johnny's imagination didn't stretch quite that far. After a moment Gracie hurried over, beaming.

"I said I was sorry I spilled the cans. And he said I'm a good girl."

"You are a good girl," Johnny said proudly, gratified to think that a month spent with him hadn't changed that fact, the way his parents thought it would.

Then he noticed Grace staring at him, probably contemplating the fact that he'd taken the rap for Gracie. After all, she "knew him when." But Grace's eyes were soft and warm and the emotion in them somehow embarrassed him. Out of earshot of Gracie he muttered, "Old grouch never gave me candy."

"He always gave licorice to me and Janelle," Grace recalled, her wistful tone telling Johnny she was missing Janelle the same as he. The sweet sharp coil of desire for her unraveled inside him, leaving a bittersweet compassion. He thought Grace's pain must be as great as his own, she and Janelle had been so close.

They left the store, following Gracie down the sidewalk. "Janelle married a great guy," Johnny said abruptly. "She was happy. But she always regretted that his work took her away from here, away from you."

"Thank you for telling me." Grace smiled up at him and he felt his heart stutter. "You can be pretty nice when you want to, Johnny Tremont."

Johnny was disconcerted to realize just how nice he wanted to be.

The three of them came to a halt by his Harley. Gracie grabbed her pink-striped helmet and Johnny winked down at her. "Gracie likes the hog, don't you, Gracie?"

Gracie gazed adoringly at Johnny. "I like the hog."

Grace didn't appear to share that sentiment. "Gracie shouldn't ride that thing down the highway. We can take my car to the farm and you can leave the bike here."

"Leave the Harley?" Was she crazy? If she'd told him to leave little Gracie, Johnny wouldn't have been more appalled. "It might get stolen."

"The police station is right over there." She pointed up the block, across the street. "Who in Ashville is going to steal it anyway? Mrs. Cromwell?"

Johnny remembered Mrs. Cromwell, the florist. The thought of her plump body, clad in a floral dress and seated on his bike, made him wince.

"If you're really worried, you could ask Eddie from the gas station to keep an eye on it."

Johnny shuddered. Eddie of the hit-and-miss repairs was the last person he wanted around his bike.

"Remember the time you hauled the Harley in Dad's truck?" Grace smiled wistfully. "I wish that old Ford still ran."

Johnny wished it did, too. He wished it was parked here right now, with the Harley loaded in back because Grace was right. He didn't want to take Gracie out on the two-lane highway on the bike. He could follow Grace along on the Harley, but he was certain little Gracie wouldn't go in the car without him.

"I'll lock up the bike and leave it." Johnny swore he felt physical pain as he did just that. He grabbed his helmet and the three of them climbed into Grace's car. They buckled Gracie in the back with her lollipop.

Johnny couldn't help but approve of Grace's little blue coupe. Like her salon, it was neat and clean. There were magnets shaped like hair bows holding small notes on the dash. One reminded her to pick up clothes from the cleaners. Another read, "C.S.— Saturday."

He frowned at the second note. A date? Grace's bare ring finger had ruled out a fiancé, but that didn't mean there wasn't a man in her life. For Gracie's sake, he was duty-bound to find out.

Checking to find Gracie busy with her lollipop and looking out the car window, Johnny tapped the note and asked idly, "Who's C.S.?"

Grace raised her brows in a what-business-of-yours-is-it? look. Most likely because he'd asked her to marry him, she deigned to answer. "A customer."

Johnny immediately relaxed. Probably one of those little old ladies who liked their hair fixed like a French poodle's.

"Chase Sinclair. He's one of my regulars." While

he stared at her, Grace braked for a stop, proceeded with caution and added casually, "We've dated a couple of times."

Johnny stared harder.

Chase. He had never liked that name. And he didn't like the familiar way Grace said it, or the unfamiliar ill humor he felt at her words. He hoped she realized that for Gracie's sake, the dates had to stop if they were to marry.

With forced nonchalance, he said mockingly, "Chase and Grace. Sounds like a cartoon."

Gracie giggled. Grace glowered. "That's juvenile, Johnny."

"You used to have a sense of humor," Johnny noted.

"I *had* to," Grace muttered. "Or I'd have been mad at you all the time." At his look of protest, she added, "Take that time you put gum in my hair."

Johnny winced, effectively chastened. Grace had had to cut bangs in her hair after that prank. Still, Johnny liked to think he'd inspired her life's work.

"And the time you scared me and Janelle when we camped on my porch."

Ah, yes. Her father had threatened to shoot until he realized who had made the girls scream. Grace and Janelle had had to sleep in the house the rest of the night. And all over a harmless garden snake.

A sense of nostalgia swept over Johnny and he suddenly missed Janelle more than ever. He caught Grace's gaze, saw the grief she couldn't quite mask. This trip down memory lane had gone on long enough. He turned in the seat. "We're almost there, Gracie."

"Why did you put gum in her hair?" Gracie asked.

"Ah..."

"Because Johnny was a tease. Does he like to tease you, too?" Grace asked.

There was a moment's pause, then little Gracie overcame her shyness to tattle. "He tickles me. But he stops if I say he has to."

"That doesn't sound like the Johnny I know," Grace murmured.

He frowned. Couldn't she see he wasn't the same person he'd been one month ago, let alone the rebellious kid he'd been as a teen? His world revolved around Gracie now.

He ran his business from Janelle's fine home, having given up his bachelor apartment. The last date he'd had was when he took Gracie to the cinema to see *Snow White*. Oddly, he hadn't missed that aspect of his life until Grace had stirred up his hormones.

Still a little surprised by that turn of events, he took a discreet survey of Grace, just testing his reaction. As she braked for the turn into the gravel lane that led to the Greens' farmhouse, Grace's skirt inched up her leg. Her skin looked silky smooth, and she wasn't even wearing stockings. The strap of her sandal around her ankle riveted his attention. He imagined his hand wrapped there, his lips there...

Johnny dragged his gaze away.

The car came to a halt as Grace parked before the

square garage. He remembered hiding in there once, after he'd sprayed Janelle and Grace with the hose. Grace had only been thirteen when he'd chased her and gotten her shirt all wet. He imagined she would look a little different now in a wet T-shirt.

"Here we are."

He jerked his gaze from Grace's shirtfront, a hot sweat breaking out on his skin. He hadn't counted on this. Hadn't counted on having sexual feelings for Grace. He wasn't going to look at her that way again, wasn't going to think about her that way. He wasn't going to marry her.

Then little Gracie climbed out of the car and cried with delight, "This is like the house in my farm book. Where are the kittens?" she asked excitedly.

Looking at Gracie's happy face, Johnny guessed he was getting married after all. But he was damn well going to keep his hands to himself. These feelings he was having for Grace seemed downright immoral.

Little Gracie was so excited, he was more than happy to crawl halfway under the porch and catch the kittens. They were a rambunctious trio of calicoes, everything Gracie could have hoped for. She sat cross-legged in the grassy shade of an elm, kittens crawling in and out of her lap.

Grace had taken the groceries into the kitchen. Johnny looked toward the house, aware this was a good time to speak privately with her, yet feeling oddly reluctant. Telling Gracie to stay put, he left the little girl with her new friends and went inside.

The house was cool and quiet, the shades drawn against the sun. He noticed the upstairs was boarded off, heard the hum of an air conditioner that hadn't been part of the house years ago. Otherwise, the place seemed unchanged.

Having moved from city to city in his early childhood, Johnny could only imagine what it must feel like to grow up and live in the same house all of your life, how it must feel to risk losing such a part of your past. Funny, how he'd only come to the Green farm to pester Grace and Janelle when he was bored, yet it was here that some of his happier memories took place.

Prints and posters of Elvis had once been framed on the walls of the hall. In the living room, the Greens had kept an old phonograph that spun forty-fives of Elvis tunes. He imagined that stuff was tucked away in the attic. He hated to think Grace would have parted with it.

Johnny wandered into the living room. A life-size poster of Elvis had once been propped in the corner, where Grace now kept a potted plant like those in her salon. Johnny grinned, thinking Elvis had more aesthetic appeal.

"When Mama was in the nursing home, we took the poster of Elvis there," Grace said from behind him as if reading his thoughts. "Dad said it kept her company."

Johnny turned to face Grace where she stood in the doorway. She looked all of fifteen again, missing her mother long before Mrs. Green had been physically gone. He said simply, "That was nice."

"Dad left it there after Mama died. Every time I go back, they've got it propped in a corner somewhere."

"You still go to the nursing home?"

"I give haircuts to some of the residents. Mama had a lot of friends there. Now they're my friends."

Johnny suspected that over the years, Grace had spent too much time at that nursing home.

But she smiled as she spoke of the people there. "Mama turned them all into Elvis freaks."

"Fans," Johnny corrected. "Fans of the King."

"Now you sound like my dad."

Johnny didn't feel like Grace's father. Right now, his thoughts probably had her dad rolling in the grave.

He shouldn't be thinking about making love with Grace. He couldn't possibly have sex with Grace.

Oh, yeah, he could.

Oh, no, he wouldn't.

He'd have to handle this carefully, he realized. He wanted Grace, and he was certain that wanting wasn't all one-sided, however reluctant Grace appeared. But she wasn't the kind of girl you had a fling with, not even a married fling.

The best way to approach this marriage, he decided, was on the basis of past friendship. No hearts involved.

And no sex.

"Where is Gracie?" Grace asked suddenly, stepping into the room.

"Playing with the kittens."

"Good. We have to figure some way short of marriage that you can keep guardianship of her."

Johnny frowned at her words, only just remembering what he'd come in here for. Then Grace walked over, stopping before him. In the dim light that filtered through the shades, she seemed suddenly, intimately close. Johnny fought to curb his adolescent reaction to her nearness. On pure reflex, he took a step back, a new dance for Johnny Tremont.

"Hold still. You've got cobwebs in your hair from crawling under the porch." Grace seemed amused and reached up to brush them away, her nearness creating a potent charge between them. When she pressed briefly against him, the snug denim over her breasts touched his chest. Johnny absorbed the shock to his system and tried not to short-circuit. With each sweep of her hand, Grace's fingers seemed to slip farther into his hair, her sweet-smelling wrist near his face, her skirt weaving about his jeans-clad legs, her sandaled feet nudging his tennis shoes. Overwhelmed, Johnny eyed the distance between Grace's mouth and his.

"You have really thick hair," Grace murmured. The brush of her fingers seemed to slow as they pushed their way through the strands. "A lot of women spend hours at the salon, trying to have hair this thick and dark."

Johnny struggled to focus his muddled thoughts.
Friends, not lovers.

A memory of dancing with Grace here in this room flashed through his mind. Sun had streamed through the window onto her shiny hair. He'd been singing along with Elvis. She'd been laughing at him. Then she'd rested her head against his shoulder, pressed her slight body to his—

I can't help falling in love…

As Johnny's hair filled her palm, Grace stilled. She was suddenly conscious of the scant space between their bodies, aware that a deep heat burned in Johnny's eyes. A longing from years ago surfaced. Grace reminded herself that Johnny was here on a mission, that he was used to having what he wanted from women. What she was feeling for him could hurt her now more than ever.

She drew back her hand, but her eyes fluttered closed as Johnny's warm breath caressed her face. She felt him anchor his hands at her waist, and for a moment she suffered conflicting fears—that he would push her away…that he wouldn't. Johnny seemed to sense the restlessness that moved through her. He touched his lips to hers gently, giving the kiss she'd imagined Johnny giving her when she was a girl.

But she wasn't a girl anymore and the sweetness of his kiss didn't soothe her. Grace only felt more restless. With his hot hands, Johnny settled her body against his. He seemed to know how, when and where to touch his lips to hers, to press her body closer, drawing a response she couldn't hide. Yearning speared through her. And yet...

She loosened the hold she'd taken on Johnny's shirtfront. But before she'd uncurled her fingers from the soft cotton, he raised his mouth from hers, his hands at her waist again, setting her away from him. Hearing the screen door slam, Grace wanted to think it was because of Gracie. But her cheeks grew hot as Johnny stepped back and shoved his hands in his pockets.

He hadn't meant to kiss her.

"Johnny!" Gracie called from the hall. "Come and see what the kittens can do!"

"I'll be right there," Johnny called in answer. The door slammed again. Johnny didn't move. But his gaze was evasive, those quick hands of his still hidden in his pockets.

Grace burned. From desire, from anger, from embarrassment. Had she only imagined those looks he'd been giving her? That tense moment in the store? Grace recalled Johnny's lack of reaction—other than to joke around—when she'd purposely mentioned dating Chase with the hope of seeing some spark of jealousy. How could she have been so foolish as to forget that he intended to pay her to marry him, that he did so because of Gracie?

So why had he kissed her?

"I'm sorry, Grace. I guess I just—I mean it's been a long time—"

That was why. Grace smiled sweetly, but she simmered inside. "Has Gracie been cramping your style?"

Johnny stilled in the act of pushing his hand through his hair. She could still feel the softness of those dark strands on her fingers. "Yeah. That explains it."

Johnny looked so relieved, Grace wanted to smack him. But Gracie was waiting outside for him, so all she said was, "Apology accepted. You'd better go see to Gracie."

"Yeah. I'll do that." Johnny turned away in unflattering haste. Then he turned back. "Gracie really does need me. She needs *us*. Just think about my offer, about the mortgage and getting married."

Johnny left the room. A moment later Grace heard the screen door softly close.

Think about us getting married.

There'd been a time when she hadn't dreamed of anything else. Then Johnny had left town and unwittingly broken her heart.

She couldn't let that happen again.

She went to the kitchen and jerked open the refrigerator door, reaching for lemonade, letting the blast of cold air chill her face before swinging the door shut.

Who else but Johnny had the nerve to return after ten years to ask a favor like marriage? Why, Johnny had no more desire to be married than he did to sell his Harley for scrap metal. As for raising a child— Grace let out a breath of disdain. Johnny had never been responsible for anything but cleaning the carburetor on his bike. That was play to him. That was why he'd made it his life's work.

Grace poured lemonade and fixed sandwiches. She plunked the glasses, along with the plates, onto a tray and marched with it out the front door. While she arranged their lunch on the redwood table, Johnny led little Gracie from beneath the tree and into the house to wash her hands.

The screen door banged behind them. Grace stared as it settled, contemplating their mission in a different light than she once would have. If Johnny had his way, he'd be responsible for making sure Gracie washed her hands until she was grown.

He probably still had trouble remembering to do so himself.

When they returned, Gracie ate quickly, wanting to get back to the kittens. When the little girl scampered over to the elm, Johnny turned to straddle the bench, resting his elbow on the table top. He watched Gracie so long, so intently, Grace thought he must have forgotten she was there. She saw the way his mouth alternately tensed and curved as he watched Gracie, the way his eyes grew light, then dark with worry. Grace's anger lifted with the breeze that ruffled through Johnny's hair.

He finally said, "Janelle was a wonderful mother, and Grant a great father. That's a tough act to follow."

She didn't detect any resentment there, just a genuine lack of confidence in his ability to raise his niece—a justifiable doubt, she had to agree. Johnny seemed to truly love little Gracie, to want this role he'd chosen in her life. But Grace couldn't help thinking of all he must have given up to do so.

"For Gracie's sake, my parents have agreed there will be no interim hearings and no scenes in front of Gracie. Still, things haven't been easy for her. I talked to her doctor and he agreed that bringing her here to the country would do her good."

As if in affirmation, Gracie held a kitten to her cheek and smiled, her eyes closing in what Grace thought must be a rare moment of peace in the recent turmoil of her young life.

"You'd be good for her, too," Johnny said quietly.

Grace filled her lungs with warm summer air. She wanted to help Janelle's child. But it was hard not to imagine having her heart broken in the process.

And, like Johnny, she lacked confidence in her ability to meet Gracie's needs. "I don't know much about kids, Johnny. I never even baby-sat when I was a teen."

"You're a woman. Child rearing is supposed to come instinctively," Johnny said with the blithe ignorance of a man.

"That's a myth. Even women have to learn about children. I've spent more time with the elderly than I have with kids."

Johnny grinned then. "Same thing. We all revert as we get older. We start watching cartoons again, start wearing bright colors. We actually decrease in size. By the time we kick the bucket, we're bald as babies and have just as many teeth.''

Grace couldn't help laughing. Johnny was irreverent. He always had been, and all the girls had been in love with him for it, herself included. But her laughter dwindled and Johnny's did, too. There was so much at stake where little Gracie was concerned.

"She wakes up at night crying." Johnny spoke as if the very image his words conjured pained him. "She cries if I leave her, afraid I won't come back."

Oh, Janelle. Tears burned Grace's eyes, for she knew little Gracie's unhappiness would break Janelle's heart. She reminded herself that Janelle was at peace in heaven with Grant. But Gracie...Gracie needed her.

"My parents won't give Gracie the love she needs," he said simply, and Grace wondered if he realized how revealing that sentiment was where he and Janelle were concerned. "And there's little chance the court will let me keep her unless I marry."

He turned to her then, more serious than she'd ever seen him. "I realize we won't have one of those one-in-a-million kind of marriages like Janelle and Grant had. But we've got friendship going for us, haven't we?"

Grace couldn't deny it. Hadn't Johnny always fixed the chain on her bicycle? Driven her and Janelle into town to see the movies?

Friends...

Johnny was watching her, his blue eyes intent and

warming her clear to that place in her heart that had always been just for him. She recognized the yearning inside her, just as she saw quite clearly that Johnny knew no such feeling, that because of his parents, he had no true concept of what love was.

He reached out and tentatively covered her hand with his atop the table. The yearning within her spread and deepened. Instinctively, Grace curled her fingers into a protective ball.

He let go of her hand. "I know it's asking a lot. But I'm asking for Gracie's sake. Will you marry me, Grace?"

A warm breeze fanned her face; the sun flashed through the tree leaves into her eyes, making them burn, making her blink.

Hadn't she seen right away that Johnny would do anything for Gracie?

Even marry her.

And Grace said softly, "Yes. I'll marry you, Johnny."

Chapter Three

She'd said "yes."

Standing on the porch with his hot palm curled around an icy glass of lemonade, Johnny watched Grace as she reclined on the grass with Gracie, playing with the kittens. He was going to be *married*. Moisture dripped from the sides of the glass onto his sneakers.

He couldn't remember ever feeling nervous over anything. Except maybe that time the police impounded the Harley...

But he felt nervous now, all those worries over being a parent compounded by the prospect of marriage—even a short-term marriage. He'd never given much thought—any thought—to either possibility until Janelle and Grant had died.

Gracie laughed out loud at something Grace whispered to her, and a sense of gratitude welled within him. No one could stay in a shell around Grace. It was like trying to stay out of the sun in a desert. He'd been right to think she could make Gracie happy.

He'd been wrong to expect she would still seem like a sister to him.

After he kissed her, he'd started to tell her how much she'd changed, and how much she hadn't, and how much the combination affected him. Thank God she'd misunderstood and thought he was suffering from sexual frustration.

Grace stretched in pursuit of a kitten, her skirt creeping tantalizingly high. Tension skittered through him. He *was* suffering from sexual frustration.

Grace settled back, and Johnny's pulse relaxed, too. He watched her and little Gracie herd kittens between them and swore once again that he would keep his hands to himself. Gracie's future depended on him. Taking a long pull of cold lemonade, he walked over and sat atop the picnic table.

"What are their names?" Gracie asked, corralling the kittens, and Johnny smiled over every word directed at Grace.

"Well...they could use good names," Grace said, and Johnny knew that she'd already named them, that she was letting Gracie give them new ones. "Do you know any good names?"

"I know the names of the Seven Dwarfs."

"All seven names?"

"Grumpy, Dopey, Sleepy, Sneezy...Doc and Happy and Bashful." Gracie scooped a wandering kitten into her hand and held it close to her face. "He's smiling. His name is Happy."

Caught up in the game, Grace picked up another kitten. "This one looks kind of Grumpy."

"No, Grumpy is the man at the store. He's..." The kitten yawned and Gracie named it appropriately. "Sleepy."

Johnny was enchanted by little Gracie as he'd never been before. Since Janelle and Grant's deaths, she'd never been this animated with others, not even when he was right there with her.

Gracie seemed to have forgotten him, seemed to have found peace. As that sense of peace flowed over him, too, Johnny realized how closely his emotions were tied to little Gracie's.

Gracie traded her kitten for the last one, who tried to hide its face ostrich-like in her hands. "He won't look at me, so he's Bashful. Grandmother Tremont calls me Bashful when I won't look at her. She said I'm just like my mother."

Johnny's serenity vanished with Gracie's words. Damn his mother's thoughtlessness. As if being like her mother was something Gracie should be ashamed of.

He was no shrink, but he figured if you told an impressionable kid she was shy too often, she would start to believe it, and to accept it. He straightened, planning to undo his mother's damage, when Grace's soft voice stopped him.

"You *are* like your mother." Johnny saw the effort with which Grace tempered her words for little

Gracie. "She was my best friend, did you know that?"

Gracie buried her face in the kitten's fur. "Johnny told me."

Johnny wanted to go to Gracie then, but Grace didn't so much as glance at him so he remained seated, trusting her instincts.

"Your mom was bashful sometimes. Most people are at one time or another. But after your mom and I got to know each other better, can you guess what happened?"

Gracie shook her head, her chin brushing over the kitten's fur.

"She wasn't so bashful. She made me laugh until we both got the giggles. She had a pretty smile, just like your smile."

Little Gracie looked up from the kitten and Johnny couldn't draw breath, waiting for her reply.

"Johnny said Mommy and Daddy are stars in heaven now. They shine on me at night."

"I'm sure they do."

Gracie went on playing with the kitten, in that way she had of revealing some emotion, then tucking her feelings away, as if that were all she could handle for the moment. Johnny let his breath ease out, then met Grace's gaze as she sat quietly with Gracie. The mixed glitter of anger and tears in her eyes assured him that whatever doubts Grace had concerning their marriage, they would not outweigh her commitment to Gracie.

After a while, Gracie called out, "Can I have a kitten at our motel, Johnny?"

"Ah..."

Grace shot him a warning look over Gracie's head and Johnny abandoned all plans to sneak a kitten into their room at the motel.

"The motel doesn't allow kittens inside," he admitted. "But you'll see them every day now that Grace and I are getting mar—"

"You can see them any day you want to," Grace interrupted, silencing him with another of those looks—as if they'd been married for years, Johnny thought wryly.

"If you'd like," she told Gracie, "you can give the kittens lunch. There's a box of food and a dish on the porch."

Gracie got up, her delight over feeding the kittens outweighing her disappointment over having to leave them at the farm. She carried Bashful, calling to the other kittens, and they trailed her across the lawn.

Grace rose and walked over with slow measured steps that were every bit as quelling as her glance had been. Johnny set his drink aside and rested his elbows on his knees, dangling his forearms in a deceptively neutral pose. When Gracie was out of earshot, Grace said, "Looks like you're still making your moves on impulse, just like you used to."

She was a picture of provocation, her hands planted at her narrow waist, her chin raised haughtily, disapproval sparking her gaze as she surveyed him. He was tempted to cuff that pert chin. Worse, he was tempted to yank her onto his lap and kiss her. Determined to do neither, he told her, "I *like* making my moves on impulse."

Grace didn't flinch and her clear green gaze packed a sexual punch that left Johnny's mouth dry.

"So I've noticed," she replied tartly. "You've spoken of our marriage in front of Gracie right from the start. You came here *assuming* I would marry you—for *money*."

Johnny, who had never blushed in his life, felt heat creep over his face. Until he'd kissed her and made her mad, he really hadn't doubted that Grace would marry him, if only for Gracie's sake. "Paying the mortgage is just my way of thanking you," he insisted.

"I don't require gratitude where Gracie is concerned. And I can pay my own mortgage." She folded her arms across her chest while Johnny silently vowed to wipe out her debt.

"I suppose you also assume I'll make all the necessary arrangements for a proper engagement and wedding."

Johnny grimaced, the word "proper" conjuring images of a formal wedding, complete with tuxes and ties. Definitely not his style. And a proper engagement didn't sound fun at all. It certainly didn't sound like anything they had time for. "Is a week long enough for a proper engagement?"

"A week?" Grace felt a flutter of panic.

"Every day counts where Gracie is concerned. Next month, when the day of the hearing arrives, the judge can't possibly give Gracie to my parents if I've—*we've*—already made a good home for her here.''

The enormity of the situation hit hard. Grace realized just how much Gracie's future depended on her. But a week? Weak-kneed, she settled beside Johnny atop the picnic table. ''Won't it seem fairly obvious to the judge why you married so suddenly—especially to a friend of Janelle's?''

''Not if my plan works right. I figure it's like being on trial. We're innocent until proven guilty, meaning they'd have to prove we're not in love. We just have to be convincing.''

''That's not a plan,'' Grace said dryly. ''That's perjury.''

''We won't have to lie. You kept in touch with Janelle over the years. The court will assume you've kept in touch with me, too. For all anyone knows, we fell in love years ago.''

His words brought a bittersweet pang to Grace's heart. Aware Johnny expected some reply, she curved her lips over the irony, her voice low as she assured him, ''They'd have a hard time proving differently.''

''Exactly. Getting married right away will also give Gracie a chance to settle in before she starts school.''

Relenting, Grace realized Johnny had thought this through carefully. Still, she couldn't help pointing out, ''You took a real chance coming all the way here with Gracie, assuming I'd marry you.''

She'd been half scolding, half setting herself up for some cheeky comment to lighten the mood. But Johnny only said with heart stopping honesty, "No, I didn't. I knew I could count on you."

And as they watched Gracie play on the porch, she silently promised that he always could.

"Just look at her," Johnny said after a while, his voice deep with pride.

And Grace had to smile at the sight of little Gracie standing on the sidewalk now, trying to coax the wayward kittens in their direction. Once, she raised her small arms in exasperation, then looked over at them and grinned. Considering Gracie, a week suddenly seemed far away.

Looking ahead, Grace realized the two big rooms upstairs would need airing out. She'd give Gracie the bedroom that faced south, so she would wake up to sunshine on fair mornings, and to the sight of the kittens on the porch steps below. The den where she herself slept downstairs would likely be converted to a temporary office for Johnny. She and Johnny would have to share the other bedroom.

Heat seemed to gather between them as Johnny's body grazed hers from shoulder to knee. Grace could feel him watching *her* now, could smell the scent of lemonade on the long slow breath he exhaled.

"I think I'd better take Gracie back to the motel now."

He rose from his perch on the picnic table. But when he called out to Gracie, telling her it was time to leave, the little girl only crouched near the kittens, refusing to look their way.

"Uh-oh," Johnny said.

"You can hardly blame her for not wanting to go back to that motel," Grace pointed out.

"What's wrong with the motel?" he asked, obviously affronted. "Gracie's got a swimming pool to play in, The Disney Channel on TV and room service. She gets clean towels and sheets every day."

Grace realized that, in his own way, Johnny was trying to take good care of little Gracie.

But a motel was no place for a child. Gracie needed to eat her meals on a table instead of a bed. She needed her own bedroom with a place to put her toys. She needed—

Grace caught herself. Maybe Johnny was right. Maybe child rearing was instinctive. On impulse, she raised her voice to ask, "How would you like to spend the night here at the farm, Gracie?"

Gracie looked up from the kittens, wide-eyed. "Can we, Johnny?"

"Uh-oh," Johnny said again.

Grace pursed her lips. Apparently, her instincts weren't too finely honed yet.

He looked smug. "You should have referred to me on that one." Then he sobered. "I don't think Gracie will stay here without me. Even if she agreed to, I don't think she would sleep through the night. Then she'll miss me."

Grace knew he was right. Even with the kittens to

entice her to stay, it was unrealistic to expect Gracie to make it through the night without Johnny near.

"I could sleep on the couch." Johnny looked down at her, his eyes dark.

Grace felt tension curl inside her. "I don't think so."

"I suppose it wouldn't be proper."

She closed her eyes over another of Johnny's lemon-scented sighs. "I'm sure it wouldn't."

"You're right." Johnny gazed down the lane. "In Chicago, my parents hired a detective to watch me, hoping to gather evidence to support their claim that I'm unfit to care for Gracie."

"Oh, Johnny." His tone was bitter, but Grace sensed the hurt there, too. She closed her eyes, envisioning Johnny as a dark-haired boy, hiding a longing for parental attention beneath his rebellion.

"We ought to just get married now."

Grace opened her eyes. *"Now?"*

"Right now. We don't have time for a big wedding anyway. Reverend Holland could marry us at the church. Just you, me and Gracie."

"I'm not sure you can arrange even that on such short notice," she said, taken aback. And she was more than a little alarmed to realize those dreams she'd once had of a beautiful traditional wedding— her and Johnny's wedding—had come back to mind, only to dissipate once more with his words.

"If Reverend Holland is still there, he won't mind," Johnny assured her.

"Don't be so sure. The last time you saw Reverend Holland he banned you from the church social,'' Grace reminded him.

"Hey, it was just a few candles."

"Johnny, we're rushing things enough already."

He grew serious suddenly. "Gracie's going to cry over leaving those kittens." His voice lowered. "I don't want to see her cry anymore."

Grace caught her lip, tenderness for Johnny and little Gracie welling inside her. She didn't want to see Gracie cry, either. And hadn't she just said that a motel was no place for the little girl? Hadn't she been thinking that for Gracie, a week was a long time?

Apparently sensing that she was weakening, Johnny got up from the table. "Come on. Let's give the Reverend a call."

"Why don't you tell Gracie? I can make the call." Grace rose slowly, suddenly nervous. Gracie wanted those kittens. But what if Gracie didn't want *her*?

They walked over, Grace pausing on the top porch stair. Johnny knelt on the sidewalk before little Gracie, taking a kitten in each hand. Her heart seemed to stop beating as she watched his lips move, telling Gracie they were going to the church so that he and Grace could marry, and how afterward the three of them would come back here to stay.

They looked up at her then, Johnny's gaze an electric blue, burning right to the core, Gracie's shy smile touching Grace's heart.

And she realized in that moment just how much she stood to lose if the Tremonts gained custody of Gracie.

Chapter Four

"We can't get married until tomorrow."

Grace stepped onto the porch, the bounce of the screen door against the frame emphasizing the silence that followed her uncertain words. As she gazed at Johnny, he was reminded of the way his mother used to look at him every summer when school got out and he was going to be home all day. A what-am-I-supposed-to-do-with-*you?* kind of look.

He didn't know whether he was more amused or insulted.

From the bottom of the steps, little Gracie's sing-song voice carried as she told each kitten she and Johnny would be sleeping here with them tonight.

A variety of sleeping arrangements passed through Johnny's mind, none of which Grace would have approved of, regardless of whether they were being watched by his parents' hired detectives. Himself on the couch, himself in Grace's bed, himself and Grace in Grace's bed…

Grace's face flushed pink, as if she was having similar thoughts, which only made it more difficult to put the brakes on *his* thoughts.

"We have to apply for the license at the courthouse before three-thirty today," she told him slowly, as if while she spoke she was still trying to decide what to do with him tonight. "We can pick it up tomorrow morning and Reverend Holland will read us our vows at the church at noon."

High noon.

Johnny noticed then that Grace was eyeing the porch swing. She surely didn't expect him to sleep outside on the porch swing.

"You can sleep on the porch swing tonight," Grace said suddenly, sounding relieved and pleased with her solution. "There's no way those detectives could use that against you."

Johnny wasn't pleased at all. "The mosquitoes will eat me alive."

"It hasn't rained for two weeks. They won't be bad." And before he could protest she added, "I have mosquito netting and repellent."

Johnny went and sat on the swing, causing it to creak, then pointedly drummed his fingers on the cushionless seat.

"I have blankets and pillows." Grace had a stubborn look on her face to match her tone and Johnny knew his protests were in vain. He was sleeping on the porch swing.

He pushed his tennis shoe against the porch floor and set the swing rocking, creaking steadily. There was something oddly comforting in the sound. Maybe it wouldn't be so bad after all. He leaned back and closed his eyes, breathing deeply. He'd missed the rich smell of country air. He remembered sitting here on summer nights harassing the girls until the dew rose. And he remembered Mrs. Green sitting here, too, holding her knitting, even when she could no longer remember how to knit.

Despite her Alzheimer's, Mrs. Green had often seemed more of a mother to him than his own. She was always here, never jetting off to some social event. It had given him a warm special feeling whenever she recognized him through the confusion her illness had caused. She never berated him over his latest prank. She'd just been glad to sit and talk with him. Him and Janelle and Grace.

"Johnny."

He opened his eyes. Little Gracie stood before him, a kitten clutched in each hand and tucked under her chin.

"I need a wedding dress," she said.

Johnny shared a smile with Grace over Gracie's confusion and explained, "The bride wears the wedding dress."

"But I want to wear a dress, too. Mommy always dressed me up for weddings."

Gracie blinked and the tears in her eyes seared Johnny's heart. Grace, it seemed, couldn't bear the little girl's unhappiness, either. She came and knelt beside Gracie. "You can wear your prettiest dress. And I'll put special flowers in your hair. Would you like that?"

Gracie nodded, but her little face remained puckered. "But Johnny didn't bring my dresses. Just my play clothes."

Uh-oh. He was in trouble now, Johnny knew. He could almost feel Grace's disapproval, her expression revealing she wasn't surprised over his blunder. To bail himself out of trouble, he offered, "I'll buy you both new dresses in town today."

"I have a dress," Grace informed him, "but we're going to find the prettiest dress in town for Gracie."

"I need shoes too," Gracie reminded them.

"Matching shoes," Grace agreed.

Gracie smiled, satisfied, and went back down the steps to the other kitten.

Johnny sighed. First the porch swing. Now shopping.

"I can take her myself," Grace offered, apparently noting his reluctance and taking pity on him.

Johnny was tempted. As taken as Gracie was with Grace, she would probably go without him. But he wasn't going to shirk his responsibilities. If he was going to raise her, he had to learn about shopping for dresses and matching shoes. He couldn't depend on Grace forever.

Johnny frowned to himself at the thought. "I'll go along," he told Grace determinedly. And because he suspected Grace wouldn't eagerly spread the news of their marriage, he added, "This will give us a chance to let it be known we're going to marry, to start building our reputation as a family.''

With his words, Grace's anticipation over shopping with Gracie evaporated. She could see Johnny was commendably bent on fulfilling his ''parental'' role with little Gracie. But his words reminded her that her part in Gracie's life was only temporary, like a part in a play. She still remembered how much she had missed being a Christmas angel after the eighth-grade Christmas play was over. Somehow, she didn't think her emotions then could compare to the way she would feel once her marriage to Johnny was over.

Gracie smiled up at her from where she sat with the kittens. Concern speared through Grace for the little girl. Johnny's views on love and marriage were so cynical that he didn't realize Gracie could come to depend on them as a unit, as her family.

But she simply couldn't tell that to Johnny, couldn't change his whole psyche with mere words. She would just have to be careful where Gracie's feelings were concerned. She would help draw the child out, but she would also take care not to let Gracie grow dependent. She wasn't going to break that little girl's heart.

But with each passing moment she was more afraid that Gracie and Johnny were going to break hers.

There was no time to dwell on her fears, though, not with their wedding set for tomorrow. The trip to the courthouse seemed to go smoothly enough, with only a few brows raised. But Grace thought they must have caused a stir after all, when Lorraine at the boutique greeted them with congratulations by the time they'd walked down the street. Mrs. Pennington at the courthouse was apparently burning up the telephone lines.

Lorraine Lawson was the same age as Johnny, and remembered him well from school. They briefly reminisced with Lorraine, who carried on about Johnny's youthful pranks, acting as if the fiasco he'd caused in the science lab with the hydrogen generator had made him a star instead of earning him a detention.

As their laughter grew louder, Grace's smile grew stiffer. When Lorraine placed her hand on Johnny's arm, swaying against him, Grace wondered how he failed to notice that Lorraine still wore her hair the same way she had in high school—blond with dark roots.

Little Gracie, who'd hidden behind Grace's skirt when Lorraine had fawned over her, now tugged on Grace's hand. Grace went willingly to look at dresses, trying to ignore the fact that Johnny didn't seem to notice.

Gracie wanted something in blue, and Grace was certain the child was inspired by pictures from Janelle's wedding album. Grace had been maid of honor and she and the other bridesmaids had worn blue. While Gracie picked out shoes, she wistfully hugged the armful of dresses Gracie had chosen to try on, lost in the memory. She gave a start at

Johnny's low voice near her ear. "How about one of these dresses for you?"

Grace turned, an emphatic "no" on her lips, when she noticed one of the many dresses Johnny held up by hangers; the lovely ivory color reminded her of her "angel" dress for the school play. Her refusal died on her lips. Then she caught sight of Lorraine hovering just behind his shoulder and said coolly, "No, thank you. I have a dress."

Her good beige linen would be fine for her pretense of a wedding.

Johnny unloaded his handful of dresses on Lorraine, who, obviously miffed, stalked away to hang them all back up. He eyed Grace closely. "Is anything wrong?"

Somewhat mollified by his easy dismissal of Lorraine, Grace said, "I was just thinking of Janelle's wedding."

A shadow passed over Johnny's face and Grace recalled how she'd missed his presence there. Janelle had explained that his absence was because of his rift with their parents, and Johnny's words confirmed it. "I should have been there. But my folks thought things might go more smoothly if I didn't attend."

Instead of bitterness, Johnny's voice was full of regret. While Janelle hadn't blamed him, Johnny had apparently blamed himself for not being there.

Unable to bear seeing Johnny so uncharacteristically down in spirit, Grace sparked his humor, noting dryly, "They were probably right."

He grinned wryly. Then he sat back in one of Lorraine's chairs to observe little Gracie in the dresses Grace helped her try on. His favorite surprised Grace with his good taste. It was an adorable ruffled pinafore, the deep blue shade of both his and Gracie's eyes. Best of all, Gracie loved it. Ruffled white socks and white patent leather shoes completed the outfit.

Once Johnny made the purchases, they left the store with plans for dinner and ice cream at the Dairy Dip just down the street.

Announcing he'd forgotten his wallet in the boutique, Johnny urged them to continue to the restaurant, then hurried back inside. Grace watched through the window as he leaned against the counter to chat with Lorraine.

Irked, Grace deposited Gracie's purchases in the car and caught Gracie's hand, grateful the little girl was willing to leave Johnny behind. She had no desire to stand and watch her soon-to-be husband flirt with Lorraine.

Once he'd joined them at the Dairy Dip, Johnny didn't seem to notice her pique; he was too busy eating and playing arcade games with Gracie. Grace was frowning into her melting milk shake when a male voice teased, "How's a guy to get a haircut when you're in here eating ice cream?"

"William! Hello. Actually, I've scheduled you an appointment at your regular time on Friday." Relieved to concentrate on someone other than Johnny, Grace fell into an easy banter with William, another of Johnny's old classmates. Or rather, she remembered uneasily, an old *adversary*.

Johnny turned at the sound of Grace's voice to find her gazing up at a blond-haired man in a suit.

Well, if it wasn't old "Bill," as Johnny had so aggravatingly liked to call him. Bill had greeted him out back of the school after his very first day at Ashville High and tried to pummel him into the football field. He hadn't liked Johnny's Harley or his leather jacket, calling him one of Hells Angels. Even more, Bill hadn't liked the attention all the girls in school were paying Johnny.

As if it was his fault he'd been irresistible.

Johnny grinned to himself at the absurdity of it. But the grin faded when Bill slipped into the booth across from Grace, shoving Johnny's milk shake aside to talk to her. Laugh with her.

Johnny frowned as she leaned her arms companionably on the table, bringing her closer to Bill. He was sure it was innocent. She couldn't possibly be attracted to Bill. Johnny had broken his nose outside of school that first day and it had healed crookedly. For a former letterman and honor society student, the guy was far from perfect.

Still, from a hired detective's point of view, Grace and Bill probably looked plenty cozy. Considering he and Grace had to present the picture of a perfect couple, Johnny could see he needed to join them. Just so no one would misunderstand, of course.

Especially Bill.

Giving little Gracie more quarters for the game she was playing, Johnny sauntered back to the table and slid into the booth beside Grace. He pressed his leg against hers then rested his arm across the low back of their booth, laying his hand on her shoulder. She shot him a look of surprise.

He was caught off-guard himself by the mesmerizing effect of her green eyes delving into his, by the warm feel of her body tucked against his while her hair swept teasingly over the top of his hand. He wanted to turn up his palm and catch the silky strands with his fingers. He wanted to take her somewhere more private, where they could be alone.

"Well, well. Johnny Tremont."

Johnny looked over at Bill, half grateful for the diversion, pleased to see that Bill's nose was still not quite straight.

Grace, however, didn't seem to think Bill looked bad at all, her eyes all warm and her smile flashing. She looked warily at Johnny. "You remember William, don't you, Johnny? He was your high school class president."

She was probably hoping he'd forgotten what a jerk Bill had been. Johnny patted her shoulder reassuringly. "Sure, I remember Bill."

"*William* is a lawyer now."

Probably made his living handling foreclosures for the bank, Johnny thought.

"I saw your old Harley parked by Grace's salon."

Johnny tensed at the disdain in Bill's voice, wondering if Bill knew that "old Harley" was worth more than the fancy car he drove. Before Johnny could find out, Grace pressed her hand on his thigh, digging in her fingernails in warning.

"How's the bike repair business going?"

"Johnny owns his own motorcycle repair and dealership now, William," Grace informed him, surprising Johnny. She almost sounded *proud* of him.

"Good for you." Bill might have been patting a child on the head for an A in spelling. "I understand congratulations are in order. I asked Grace to dinner, only to find out she's getting married tomorrow."

Johnny didn't like the shrewd look in "William's" eye, especially the way it strayed to little Gracie. He imagined Bill more easily now as a divorce lawyer, thriving on custody battles. A sense of protectiveness for his niece surged through him, a feeling Grace seemed to share as she stiffened beside him. Johnny tightened his arm around her and held Bill's gaze as he said evenly, "That's right."

"I wish you the best of luck," Bill told Grace, sounding as if he thought she would need it. Then he rose from the booth, making a show of straightening his lawyer's tie. "Well, some of us still have to work for a living. Great seeing you again, Tremont. And I'll see you at the salon, Grace. Friday morning, eleven sharp."

Johnny watched Bill walk out of the Dairy Dip. First "Chase," now "William." He guessed he wasn't the only man to notice how Grace had blossomed since she was a teen.

How was it she'd never married, he wondered again, gazing down at her. She was definitely the type to buy into the hype of wedded bliss, and maybe even make it work, the way Janelle had. Grace's work at the salon, combined with her effort to keep the farm after her father's fatal heart attack, must have kept her from much of a social life. He was glad to think he could help where the farm was concerned. But there was really no way to repay her for all she was doing for Gracie.

Prepared to scold Johnny, Grace was flustered by the warmth that came into his eyes. He didn't seem to notice that he'd filled his hand with her hair, his fingers caressing it gently. Then he lowered his gaze to her hand, and Grace realized she no longer gripped his leg in warning, that instead she'd spread her hand warmly upon his thigh. They each drew back abruptly as little Gracie came over to the table.

"I want to go play with the kittens," Gracie said, crawling into the booth and onto Johnny's lap, obviously tired from shopping. While he promised Gracie they would pick up her things and return to the farm, Grace knew she should follow through and scold Johnny, well aware he'd been on the verge of drawing William into a fight. But Johnny was cuddling little Gracie so sweetly, and the warmth of his gaze lingered. She was certain there had been something more than gratitude in his eyes.

But that was only wishful, foolish thinking, the kind she'd given up on long ago.

Pushing such thoughts from her mind with renewed determination, Grace walked with Johnny and Gracie to the car. Johnny buckled little Gracie in back amid giggles and whispers. Grace drove to the motel. At Johnny's insistence, she waited in the car with Gracie while he ran in to gather Gracie's things. They'd decided Johnny would come back in the morning to pick up their license, then dress for the wedding, check out and bring his belongings to the farm.

Grace pressed her lips wryly. Johnny probably hadn't wanted her to see the mess inside the motel room. She considered for the first time what it would be like having Johnny and little Gracie living in her house. What it would be like having a man around.

Fortunately, they were on their way before those thoughts became any more vivid. Gracie was amenable to the idea of Johnny riding ahead of them on his bike, so they swung back by the salon. Grace hurried in to make a phone call to her co-worker, Marcy, to determine the shifting of tomorrow's appointments in her absence.

Aware Grace dated only rarely, Marcy was surprised by the sudden marriage, and more than a little suspicious of Johnny. And Marcy didn't even know Johnny from before, having only moved to Ashville this past year. Considering Marcy's protective, bigsister attitude, Grace wondered how her and Johnny's first meeting would go.

But despite having misgivings, Marcy offered to take over some of the appointments and to reschedule the rest, leaving Grace to concentrate on her ''special day.'' She hung up the phone and walked slowly outside. If Marcy only knew…

Following Johnny to the farm was a sweet kind of torture for her, watching his long legs molded to the sides of the Harley, the muscles in his tanned arms flexing as he wound the bike out, the roar of the engine building, the sound reaching back to her. When he pulled off the helmet at the farm, thick strands of his hair, shiny from sweat, laced his forehead. He grinned at her, as bright-eyed as a kid with a new bicycle.

Ignoring the magical pull of those eyes, Grace went to open the door. While little Gracie played with the kittens, she and Johnny opened up the second story of the house, turning off the air conditioner and letting the late-day breeze flow through the screens. She cleaned the upstairs bathroom and did some hasty dusting in Gracie's room.

As she placed little Gracie's play clothes in the dresser, she tried not to dwell on where Johnny's clothes would go once he brought them here. He'd gone downstairs, and now she wondered what he and Gracie were up to. The house was far too quiet.

Then she heard Johnny's steps behind her.

"Here." Johnny shoved a white box under her nose.

Lorraine's Boutique. Grace read the embossed label and frowned, perplexed. She'd already hung Gracie's dress in the closet.

"Take it. Open it."

Because Johnny seemed so eager for her to do so, Grace took the box and went to sit on the bed. She ran her fingers over the gold letters. It had been a long time since she'd had a present. No family nearby, Janelle gone, no man in her life to romantically lavish her with presents...

She looked up at Johnny. Brows furrowed, he pushed his hands into his jeans pockets and rocked on the heels of his tennis shoes, a picture of impatience.

No man to romantically lavish her with presents...

She realized Johnny had bought her a dress, despite the fact that she'd told him not to. Grace fought the flutter of her heart, the warmth that stole over her. Johnny was still trying to make up for his oversight in not packing Gracie's dresses, she decided. She pressed her lips, imagining Lorraine guiding him through his purchase, probably making the choice for him. More than likely there was some hideous, unflattering dress in the box.

"Look, if you don't want it, just say so."

Johnny was out-and-out scowling now. In a move totally out of sync with her thoughts, Grace clutched the box tighter. "I'll open it."

And if it turned out to be as awful as she thought, she would take it right back to Lorraine and—

Grace's cold thoughts melted away as pleasure flowed over her at the sight of the ivory dress. Her angel dress. Her hands slid over the silky, lace-trimmed fabric. Lorraine would never have chosen this for her.

"It reminded me of the dress you wore in that Christmas play Janelle dragged me to," Johnny said earnestly, as if she needed convincing that the dress would suit her. "Remember? You had on wings and wore a red ribbon in your hair."

Grace remembered. He'd teased her unmercifully about her green eyes and that red ribbon, telling her she looked more like a Christmas elf than an angel. What she couldn't believe was that Johnny remembered that night, too.

But then, aside from the influence of his hormonal urges, wasn't that how he still saw her? As the girl she'd once been?

Johnny was grinning, but the grin slipped a little as she sat in silence, desperately trying not to make too much of the fact that he could recall this small thing about her, in the same way that she could recall every passing moment, every touch, every look, *everything* about him since the day he'd first grinned at her.

"I figure if you skip the red ribbon, the dress should look okay for a wedding. At least it's white, and you must have liked that color—"

"Ivory. The dress is ivory. And it's lovely, Johnny, thank you." She managed a smile that was not overly grateful, not too revealing of the impact his gift had on her. It wasn't as if she was still in love with him....

"Yeah, well, I had to do something to convince Lorraine I was taken," Johnny said wryly.

Grace suspected her answering laugh was lacking, but fortunately little Gracie chose that moment to run into the room. Gracie clutched Johnny's leg, peeked over at her and whispered, "Does she like it?"

"She thinks it's perfect, don't you, Grace?"

"Yes, I do."

"Johnny hid it in the car while we were at Dairy Dip, and I didn't tell." Gracie seemed to have enjoyed her part in Johnny's secret—almost as much as Johnny did. He was smiling again, that grin he used to grin after he'd gotten away with mischief.

Grace caught herself smoothing her fingers over the silk and knew if she wasn't careful, Johnny would get away with a lot more than that. Placing the lid on the box, she followed Johnny and Gracie out of the room.

The upstairs was still too stuffy for sleeping, so they opened the sofa downstairs into a bed. It was near the window by the porch swing and Gracie seemed content to share the bed with Grace, knowing Johnny was just outside.

A cool breeze sifted through the screen. Crickets sang by moonlight. Dressed in comfortable shorts and a T-shirt, Grace lay beside little Gracie, listening as the child whispered to Johnny, who whispered back, the swing creaking now and again when he moved.

Grace caught the scent of bug repellent, and heard the rustle of mosquito netting. She smiled, but her heart ached as she recalled the pain in Johnny's voice when he'd told her he didn't want to see Gracie cry anymore. Johnny loved his niece wholeheartedly, as purely and unaffectedly as a child himself. If he ever fell in love with a woman, he would love her with all his heart, as well.

Reminding herself that Johnny didn't believe in that kind of love, Grace lay listening to whispers in the dark that would haunt her long after Johnny and Gracie were gone.

Chapter Five

Grace woke the next morning to a thud outside the living room window. The chains holding the porch swing chinked like wind chimes. Johnny swore. Careful not to wake little Gracie, she rose up to look through the screen at the man she was going to marry today.

Johnny sat on the floor, rubbing his head, his bare tanned arm extended from his equally bare sun-burnished torso. As he pushed his fingers into his hair, taut muscle rode over his lean rib cage and flexed across his shoulders.

His jeans were unsnapped, and her favorite blue quilt was tangled about his long legs and bare feet. Grace breathed shallowly, her heart racing. Maybe she was still dreaming...

Johnny met her gaze then, the swing settling against his back as he stared at her. Deep and dark, desire twisted inside her, a wanting unlike anything she'd felt while loving Johnny when she was fifteen. That had been puppy love. This was—

Lust, Grace thought in a panic. And her panic rose as she saw an answering desire darken Johnny's eyes. He flung off the quilt and scooped his white T-shirt from the porch floor, shoving his arms through the sleeves and pulling it over his head. When he looked up again, his gaze was impassive, the heat gone from his eyes.

Johnny shook his disheveled hair into place, not bothering to snap his jeans, just tugging down the hem of his T-shirt. Conscious now of her tousled hair and faded floral T-shirt, Grace curled her hands into fists where she rested them atop the sofa bed, her face burning, her heart beating dully. She was going to have to do better—not to forget, even for a moment, that Johnny didn't really want this marriage, didn't want *her.*

Grace gave a start as little Gracie popped up on the bed, her pink blanket tucked under her chin. Her sleepy eyes widened at the sight of Johnny sitting on the porch floor. "Did you *fall?*"

"Sure did." Finished tying his shoes, Johnny got up and walked over to the screen, shoving his hands into his jeans pockets. It took all of Grace's willpower not to dwell on the fact that those jeans were unsnapped beneath his T-shirt.

"Did it *hurt?*"

Gracie's concern for Johnny was based on the child's very real fear for him, Grace knew. She smoothed her hand comfortingly over the child's hair as Johnny leaned close to the screen. "Not a scratch."

Which was the truth, though Grace thought Johnny might have a pretty good bump on his head.

"I'm going to town to clean up and pick up the marriage license," he told them.

Gracie pressed her nose to the screen. "We need wedding flowers for my hair."

"I'll take care of that," Johnny said, giving Gracie's nose a tap through the screen. "You girls can get gussied up while I'm gone."

Grace didn't miss the uncertainty that clouded the little girl's face as Johnny crossed the yard, pulling the keys she had given him last night from his pocket before climbing into her car. She caught little Gracie's hand, determined to keep her too busy to miss Johnny. "How about we cook pancakes, then make you a bubble bath?"

After breakfast and Gracie's bath, she got out her mother's jewelry box and settled Gracie on the sofa bed to play with it, the way she herself had as a child. Her father had never been able to buy real stones or precious metal, but he'd given what he could out of love, and her mother had never seemed to want more. Little Gracie seemed to think she had found treasure, and Grace smiled wistfully, certain her parents would have approved of this marriage for Gracie's sake, perhaps all the more if it had been real.

While Gracie played, she took a quick shower. She'd carried her clothes and cosmetics up from the den while Gracie was bathing, careful not to leave her alone for too long. Smiling now at the sound of Gracie singing downstairs, she decided she'd better live up to the little girl's image of a bride. She fluffed up her bangs and swept her hair into a loose bun, leaving stray wisps to brush at her cheeks.

After she'd slipped into the ivory dress, she hesitated, pivoting before the mirror. It fit perfectly. In fact, there was something almost...*sexy*...in the way the silk clung to her curves. But that was probably only her imagination. After all, the dress had reminded Johnny of her "angel" dress.

Grace took one last look in the mirror. This time, she saw the chaste reflection of a bride and for a moment had the heart of a girl, full of hopes and dreams. But her dreams hadn't come true, and she knew better than to let those hopes take root.

Little Gracie's excited voice drifted upstairs as she greeted Johnny. A sense of rightness came over Grace that transcended all regrets and misgivings. Nothing seemed to matter more in that moment than to ensure Gracie's happiness.

It was then that she realized she'd forgotten to specify a color and type of flower for Johnny to buy for Gracie's hair. She hurried toward the stairs. Johnny had chosen her dress based on one she had worn when she was a schoolgirl. For all she knew, he might have come back with the orange tiger lilies she and Janelle used to pick alongside the road.

She started downstairs, wincing over the image of orange flowers with Gracie's blue dress—

Her steps halted midway at the sight of Johnny standing at the bottom of the stairs. Dressed in a navy suit, bearing ivory roses, a price tag still hanging from the cuff of his jacket, he literally stole her breath away.

He'd apparently heard her coming, and grimacing at the flowers he held, he muttered, "Hope these are okay."

Grace thought they were perfect. And so did little Gracie, judging by the way she stood on the toes of her patent leather shoes to sniff the blooms. Grace continued down the stairs, trying not to dwell on the fact that Johnny had probably had lots of practice buying flowers for his women acquaintances in Chicago.

"Back in Chicago, one of the guys at the garage had a mother who was a florist." He was still frowning at the flowers. "But I picked these out myself."

Grace caught her lip. That bit of information shouldn't make her heart leap. After all, the flowers were for Gracie.

Ivory roses tied with blue ribbon. And white baby's breath. She could make a wreath for Gracie's hair and let Gracie carry the rest. After Johnny handed a bouquet to Gracie, she realized he still held a bouquet in his hand. For her.

Oh, Johnny. Grace took the bouquet Johnny held out and brought the fragrant petals to her nose. "These are lovely."

"Yeah, real pretty."

She raised her head and wondered if she was destined to spend what time she and Johnny were married trying not to take every look he gave her to heart. But Johnny was staring at *her*, not the roses now, as if he really did think she looked pretty, as if the dress seemed sexy to him, too.

Better to concentrate on that tag still attached to Johnny's sleeve, to remember that Johnny was suffering from an acute case of celibacy these days. Setting aside her flowers, Grace found scissors in the small hall desk. Taking hold of Johnny's sunbrowned wrist, trying to ignore the clean male scent of him and fighting the rush every woman feels standing near a man wearing a tie that begs to be loosened, she snipped off the tag.

"So, is the suit okay?" he asked, tugging at the knot of his tie.

"It's fine." He looked as if he was wearing one of the designer labels he could afford. But Grace suspected he didn't know the difference between the department store special he wore and an Armani, his taste running more to T-shirts.

And roses...

Grace wove a wreath for Gracie to wear as a crown. Gracie insisted she wear flowers, too, and Grace held her breath while Johnny tucked a small bloom in her hair. He stepped back. She let out her breath. It was time to go.

Reverend Holland greeted them outside the small white church that stood on the outskirts of town, much the same as he'd greeted the folks of Ashville for Sunday services the past thirty years.

"I hear you've done well for yourself, Johnny Tremont." The white-haired reverend extended his plump hand for a handshake with Johnny. Then, sounding like old Henry Gold, he added wryly, "I also heard you were in jail."

This time, Johnny had the grace to look sheepish.

"No, sir. And I don't intend to be. I've mended my ways."

Reverend Holland smiled contemplatively at little Gracie. "So I see."

Grace clutched her roses tightly. She suspected from his thoughtful expression that the reverend had the whole scenario figured out. She braced herself for a lecture on the true meaning of matrimony, and was surprised when Reverend Holland clasped his hands together and welcomed them into the church.

It was hushed and lovely inside. Grace was glad Johnny had opted against a courthouse marriage— but only because little Gracie would have been disappointed. Gracie followed the reverend down the aisle, her steps halting as she gazed up and around at the beautiful stained glass windows. At the altar they greeted the reverend's wife and a church worker who'd agreed to be their witness. The reverend had Gracie stand beside him so that she could watch as Grace and Johnny took their vows.

The ceremony was simple, timeless. They vowed to love, honor and cherish one another—just as Grace had once secretly promised she would do. Now she made the promise for Gracie's sake, as she knew Johnny did. But when Johnny caught hold of her hand, Grace felt a rush of old feelings for him that had nothing to do with the child.

She struggled to focus on the reverend's words.

"You may place the ring on her finger...."

Grace looked down at her left hand. Johnny was slipping a ring on her finger. An exquisite gold band of inlaid diamonds. Janelle's ring...

Tears filled her eyes and the stones blurred into one giant sparkle. Johnny had sent Janelle this ring as a graduation gift, and Janelle had apparently willed it back to him. Now, as Johnny gave the ring to her, she couldn't help but feel her friend's hand in this marriage. Janelle was the only person who had known of her love for Johnny.

She was going to cry, so Johnny squeezed Grace's trembling hand. It was easy to see that the ring turned her thoughts to Janelle, just as it had done for him. But he wanted Grace to have it, knew Janelle would have wanted this too. Almost desperately now, he gripped her hand, willing Grace to keep the ring. When Janelle had died, he hadn't expected ever again to feel this close to another person.

"I pronounce you man and wife."

The feeling of closeness seemed to blossom and spread with the tremulous smile Grace gave him. It transformed completely when the reverend said succinctly, "And now you may kiss the bride."

He was *married*. Something he'd never thought he would be. He ought to be going into shock. But all he could think was that tonight was his wedding night. That Grace—beautiful, sexy Grace—was his bride. That he wanted to do more than just kiss her...

Forgetting little Gracie, forgetting the reverend, Johnny pulled Grace into his arms and kissed her. Kissed her until he felt her kissing him back.

The reverend cleared his throat loudly. As she jerked away, Grace pushed her fistful of flowers into his solar plexus. Breathless, he realized little Gracie was staring at him, her blue eyes wider than the first time he'd taken her for a spin on the Harley.

"That was a *big* kiss," Gracie observed with what Johnny referred to as a child's ability to call a spade a spade. His lips were still burning and Grace's cheeks were bright pink.

Mrs. Holland eased them past the moment, reappearing with a small wedding cake, which they shared in the reverend's office. Talk was steered safely along the lines of Sunday school for Gracie, the reverend going so far as to invite Johnny to attend a church social.

Johnny felt forgiven, but not distracted. As they left the church, he noticed how the lacy hem of Grace's dress brushed her calves, drawing his eye to her delicate ankles, how lace dipped down the front of the dress to the tantalizing curve of her breasts. He was sure the row of tiny front buttons had been put there just to torment him. All this from a dress he'd bought because it was the color of the one Grace had worn in school, the one that had made her look so angelic—never mind that he'd called her a green-eyed elf.

Grace *did* look angelic, Johnny admitted to himself as he drove. Soft ivory dress, softer-looking ivory skin. But she also looked sexy, and there lay the problem. How was he supposed to get through the nights—especially his wedding night—with her looking like that and him feeling like this? Maybe he'd better sleep on the porch swing again.

Grace was apparently having the same thought. When they arrived at the farm, and while little Gracie lingered outside to greet the kittens, she asked, "Do you really think Gracie will expect us to share the same room like her parents did?"

Johnny sure as hell hoped not. Sharing the small space of the hall, with the sun glowing gold through the screen door on Grace's brown hair and silhouetting her curves beneath silk, was torture enough. "Grant was gone a lot on business. Maybe she won't—"

Gracie came inside then, her patent leather shoes tapping on the hardwood floor, the ruffles of her pinafore bouncing. She stopped near the suitcases Johnny had left in the corner. "I want to help carry."

So saying, Gracie grabbed his tennis shoes. She carted them up the stairs, turning into Grace's bedroom, leaving Johnny to stare after her, wondering if sex education began in preschool these days.

From upstairs, the shoes thudded on the hardwood floor of Grace's room.

Johnny glanced at Grace standing beside him. "Uh-oh."

Grace traced her tongue across her lip uncertainly. Johnny wanted to trace her lips, too....

"Gracie won't know the difference if you sleep on the sofa." She sounded as if she wanted desperately to believe that. She was probably still a little unnerved by the attraction she felt for him, Johnny thought. She'd been waiting for Mr. Right, yet here she was, married to Mr. Wrong. And while her hesitance sent his hormones into overdrive, he knew— married or not—he couldn't take advantage of the fact that Grace felt desire for him too.

Gracie reappeared at the top of the stairs, and Johnny hefted his suitcases in his hands. In an aside to Grace he whispered, "We'll just follow her lead until she goes to bed."

But even after two readings of *Snow White and the Seven Dwarfs,* Gracie couldn't seem to settle down that night, needing a hug or a drink or to find her blanket every ten minutes or so. Run ragged from trips up and down the stairs, Johnny and Grace finally stayed upstairs, Johnny insisting Grace get some sleep before work tomorrow. Because it was obvious he was going to have to remain within earshot of little Gracie, they agreed he would spread the blankets Grace gave him over the floor for a bed once Gracie had fallen asleep.

Johnny sat on the edge of little Gracie's bed until she quieted. She had her pink blanket tucked under her chin and lay curled on her side, sleeping in the shine of the stars he'd shown her out the window. She looked as fragile as one of Janelle's china dolls, and he felt the full weight of his responsibility, along with a deepening gratitude to Grace. He wasn't alone in this—at least not for now.

Rising slowly, so as not to disturb Gracie, Johnny crossed the hall. Little Gracie's restlessness had served one good purpose; it had kept the prospect of sharing his bride's bedroom at the back of his and Grace's minds.

But while Grace had finally fallen into a fitful sleep, Johnny was left to watch her stir and tangle the sheets around her slender legs, her hair fanning over the pillow beneath her head. He leaned in the doorway, tucking his restless hands into the pockets of his gray gym shorts. Wearing her faded floral T-shirt, big enough to fit him, with baggy green shorts, she looked sexy enough to have a sweat breaking out over his body, dampening his gray T-shirt.

It was probably because what showed of her legs was silky and smooth, her shorts riding up just enough to tantalize. Or maybe it was because her shirt had fallen slack over her enticingly bare shoulder. Moonlight flowed over her like a white blanket that revealed more than it covered, while the breeze through the screen brushed her silky bangs across her forehead. Her delicate lashes shadowed her cheeks like dark crescent moons.

This afternoon, Grace had been beautiful with her hair swept up in a way that made a man want to seduce her into letting it down. She'd tempted him then, and she tempted now as she slept. Grace was twenty-five, and probably not inexperienced. He knew that she wanted him.

He also knew Grace deserved all those promises he didn't believe in.

She curled on her side, sighing softly in the quiet night. Johnny caught the hem of his T-shirt and pulled it over his head. He spread out his blankets and lay down. Linking his hands behind his head, he listened to the soft rustle of wind-stirred tree leaves, their shadows swaying on the moonlit walls.

He was intensely aware of each murmur, each movement Grace made in her sleep. Someday she would know the kind of love Janelle and Grant had shared. The kind her parents had had, staying together through good times and bad. The kind of love he hadn't believed possible....

Sometime in the night, Johnny came awake abruptly. He'd turned on his side in his sleep, and now, below the ruffled pink hem of Gracie's Snow White nightgown, he found ten tiny toes lined up by his nose. Behind him, on the bed, he could hear Grace rousing, pushing the sheet aside. That they might have a predicament here occurred to Johnny as little Gracie crouched beside him, clutching her pink blanket.

"Did you *fall?*" Gracie asked, just as she had when he'd fallen from the porch swing.

"Sure did," Johnny answered, just as he had then. But this time he lowered one hand behind him and crossed his fingers. He looked over his shoulder to find Grace grinning sleepily at him.

For a moment, he forgot about little Gracie, entranced by the sight of Grace, her hair tousled, her face flushed, her rumpled shirt hanging off her shoulder again. She looked like she'd just had sex.

Really great sex.

"Johnny?"

He whipped his gaze back to Gracie.

"I can't sleep." Gracie rested her chin on her blanket, her eyes tired. And much too sad for a little girl's eyes to be.

"Come on, then." Johnny rose, gathering up Gracie as he did. "I'll tuck you back in."

Gracie looped her small arm about his neck. "I want to sleep in here with you and Grace."

"Ah…" The picture that came into Johnny's mind of himself in Grace's bed somehow failed to include little Gracie.

At a loss for words, he turned to Grace. She wasn't grinning now. Or sleepy. She just seemed sort of…alarmed, hitching her T-shirt onto her shoulder.

"Mommy and Daddy let me in bed when I couldn't sleep."

With little Gracie's words, everything about Grace seemed to soften. She edged over in the bed and patted the mattress. "Come here."

Gracie gave a happy bounce in his arms and Johnny carried her over, making a production of swinging her onto the bed. She scooted next to Grace, careful to leave room for him.

That space in the bed, just for him, left a warmhearted feeling inside Johnny. Still, he hesitated. It was Grace's bed, Grace's call. She gave him a wry grin and told little Gracie, "You'd better hang on to Johnny so he won't fall."

So Johnny crawled into bed to the accompaniment of Gracie's giggles, as she snuggled in the curve of his arm. As he settled in, his arm brushed against Grace's smooth arm. He was surprised not to see static sparks in the darkness from the contact before Grace jerked away in reflex. Oblivious, little Gracie yawned and tucked her blanket under her chin.

Resigned to a night of suffering over Grace, Johnny stared at the ceiling. But the moonlight held a magnetic pull that drew his gaze to the beams that shone over her and little Gracie.

Grace's flowered shirt rose at her breasts with each breath she took. Her eyes were closed, her silky lashes dark against cheeks painted porcelain by the moonlight. He caught the scent of lemon from her shampoo and for a moment, he saw himself back on the Greens' front porch, back in time, drinking lemonade with the Greens and Janelle and Grace....

He felt a churning inside himself, not sharp like desire, but deep like a *need*. Then little Gracie reached in her sleep for Grace, resting her small hand on Grace's arm, and his restlessness seemed to ebb. And soon he fell into a sleep that was as contented as little Gracie's.

But the tension only intensified for Grace as she lay awake, aware of little Gracie touching both her and Johnny, forming a connection she felt clear to her once broken heart.

Chapter Six

Morning brought the soft glow of sun outside the window and a dew-freshened breeze wafting in to tease Grace awake. Eyes closed, she quietly savored the comforting warmth of sharing her bed with little Gracie and Johnny, lulled by the soft rhythmic sounds of their breathing. She caught the childhood scent of No More Tears shampoo, but it was the bolder masculine scent of Johnny that seemed to dominate the chaste blue-and-white room that had been hers from birth.

Lying on her side, precariously near the edge of the mattress, she blinked sleepily. She smiled at the incongruous sight of little Gracie's pink ruffled gown draped over Johnny's tan, muscled forearm as he curled his arm around his niece. For someone not used to sharing her bed, she'd slept soundly with

Gracie and Johnny taking up three quarters of the mattress.

Grace nestled her head upon her curved arm. She'd once imagined what it would be like to lie beside Johnny Tremont in bed. The reality, even with little Gracie between them, was far better than anything she had imagined when she was fifteen. Her pale blue sheets contrasted beautifully with his black hair and sun-bronzed skin. He needed a shave, but the shadow over his lips held Grace momentarily entranced. His legs stretched beyond hers, and made her feel delicate, feminine. Made her imagine how her body would fit pressed beneath his...

Alerted by the change in the rise and fall of Johnny's chest, Grace jerked up her gaze. Johnny's eyes glinted unmercifully. He carefully leaned past little Gracie until his face was close to hers. The mattress dipped as he braced his hand at her side, his knuckles pressing against her waist through her T-shirt. Grace caught a quick breath and lay back against her pillow, fully awake now, her body pulsing with reaction to his.

"Gracie slept through the rest of the night," Johnny whispered, reminding Grace that it was uncommon for Gracie to do so. A tender, protective feeling for the little girl washed over her.

"Will she be all right when she wakes?" Grace whispered back. Though she couldn't bear the thought, she wanted to be ready if little Gracie woke, crying for Janelle.

"We'll remind her first thing about those kittens. She'll be okay."

Johnny leaned closer, making Grace uncomfortably aware that her face was scrubbed clean as Gracie's, that her hair was spread over the pillow in every direction, and that she wasn't wearing a bra beneath her T-shirt. Johnny parted his lips, his breathing shallow, and unconsciously, Grace parted hers, breathing in sync. Johnny blinked. Grace blinked. Was it only her imagination or was he lowering his mouth to hers?

Between them, little Gracie stirred.

"Thanks for sharing your bed." Johnny's warm breath whisked upon Grace's lips and his voice came huskily through the ringing in her ears. Then he drew back his arm and leaned away in time for Gracie to sit up between them.

"Hey, look, it's Snow White," Johnny teased, apparently unruffled by the close proximity that left Grace's heart beating erratically as she scooted up in the bed and propped herself against the headboard.

Gracie looked at each of them in turn, then pursed her lips at Johnny. "I'm not Snow White. It's me, *Gracie.*"

"It says *Snow White* on your dress. Right there." Johnny tickled Gracie.

When the little girl squealed and bounced toward her, Grace hugged her close, unable to resist pressing a kiss to Gracie's shiny dark hair.

"This isn't a dress, it's my *nightgown,*" Gracie corrected from the safety of Grace's arms.

"Why, so it is." Johnny cocked his head toward the window, as if listening. "I think I hear a hungry kitten."

Gracie's mouth popped open. "They want me to feed them."

"Well, let's go feed them." Apparently unhindered by the fact that Gracie was, indeed, wearing a nightgown, Johnny held out his hand. Gracie scrambled from bed, pulling Grace along. Grace noticed that Johnny seemed to find it amusing, watching her hitch her shirt onto her shoulder and tug down the legs of her shorts while climbing after Gracie. Grace sighed inwardly. Johnny probably found her attraction to him amusing as well, just as he would have when they were teens.

They trooped down the stairs and Grace had to smile as little Gracie hurried through the door Johnny opened, her bare feet patting across the sun-warmed boards of the porch. Three calico kittens struggled up the steps to greet her. The ruffles of Gracie's gown brushed the dusty porch floor as she squatted to carefully pour cat food into their dish.

Looking pleased, Johnny crossed his arms and leaned in the door beside Grace. Little Gracie's delight and Johnny's nearness gave her a feeling of contentment she knew better than to get used to.

With reluctance, she straightened. "I'll make breakfast, then get ready for work."

"Gracie and I will make breakfast for you," Johnny told her. And Gracie jumped up from beside her kittens at the prospect.

But the prospect only made Grace wary. She'd never known Johnny to be much of a cook. But little Gracie was excited, already catching Johnny's hand to lead him back into the kitchen. To make breakfast for *her*.

Touched, Grace made her way upstairs to shower. She slipped into a neat khaki short set for work, but it only made her feel like spending a day at the town park instead of in the salon. Little Gracie would love the swings and slide there. The rope on the old tire swing on the farm had frayed, but Grace decided right then to have Johnny rehang it.

She returned downstairs and headed toward the kitchen, trying to remember if there was rope in the garage or the barn—

Oh, my.

Her kitchen...

It looked as if it had snowed on the kitchen table. It looked as if a dozen guests had piled dirty dishes in the sink. It looked as if there had been a fire.

"I've got everything under control," Johnny said.

Standing in front of the stove, he waved a spatula to clear the haze. "Bacon's almost done."

The sight of her yellow kitchen towel tucked at the waist of Johnny's low-slung gym shorts, his bare torso gleaming above them, served to distract Grace. She felt Johnny's gaze burning a path over her body from the sandal straps at her ankles to the vee of her shirt collar. Stepping over to the table, she gingerly scooped eggshells into her hand, broken pieces that would symbolize the remnants of her heart if she wasn't careful. "Where is Gracie?"

"I sent her out to play with the kittens while I—uh—aired out the kitchen."

With Gracie still in her nightgown, no doubt.

Johnny set down the spatula. He went over and lifted the garbage pail, bringing it to the table. With his arm, he cleared the table in one sweep, leaving only a cloud of flour behind. "There we go. And don't worry. I'll do the dishes."

"That would be good." Grace dropped her shells into the garbage pail, brushed flour dust from her shorts and wistfully thought how she usually had toast for breakfast.

Little Gracie appeared at the kitchen door then. Seeing Grace, she said shyly, "I made pancakes."

Faced with the disaster of a kitchen, Johnny cursing softly at the stove, little Gracie with bare dirty feet and flour on her nightgown, Grace thought she hadn't felt so needed in a long time. She smiled at Gracie. "Pancakes are my favorite breakfast."

While Johnny put the "finishing touches"—whatever they might be—on breakfast, Grace took little Gracie to wash up and dress. As they started downstairs, Grace couldn't help but wonder how Johnny was going to cope with another meal at lunchtime, plus watch Gracie, all the while trying to rearrange the den into an office.

Once in the kitchen, though, Grace discovered part of Johnny's plan: he had set the table with paper plates.

Grace didn't have the heart to remind Johnny, who had thankfully dressed for the meal in his gray T-shirt, that the everyday dishes were in the kitchen cupboard. She simply enjoyed her breakfast, probably too much so, considering the bacon was burned and the pancakes cold.

When it came time to leave and Johnny stood with her on the porch promising to get the den converted, worry crept over Grace again. He had probably given no thought to how easily Gracie might wander off after a kitten while he was setting up his office or making a business call. Children disappeared all the time. Maybe she should stay...

"Shouldn't you be going?" Johnny asked as she lingered.

"I was thinking I should stay home today and help you fix up the den." That way, she could keep an eye on Gracie.

"There's no need. I can manage. Gracie can help me when she's not too busy playing with those kittens." He grinned. Gracie was chasing the kittens about the grassy yard as he spoke.

"I really wouldn't mind helping."

Noting the close way Grace watched little Gracie play, Johnny guessed she was enjoying her role as parent and hated to leave. But he understood Grace had a business to run. "There's no need." Teasingly he added, "You'd better go before the boss fires you."

Grace's answering smile seemed distracted. And

she was twisting her purse strap into a knot, as if she was fretting over something.

Her gaze flickered his way and Johnny realized the something she fretted over was *him*.

He frowned. Grace suffered from more than a reluctance to leave little Gracie. It was more like a reluctance to leave Gracie with *him*, as if she was leaving two four-year-olds alone instead of an adult and a child.

She must have noticed his indignation. For a moment, her chin came up and Johnny braced himself. Judging by the look in her eye and his mounting temper, they were going to have their first fight.

But Grace simply said, "Make sure Gracie stays in the yard. There's poison ivy out by the fence line. And the barn—don't let her wander inside alone...."

Johnny folded his arms across his chest. Grace pressed her lips and descended the porch steps, walking toward Gracie who abandoned the kittens with the realization that Grace was leaving. The two engaged in a long conversation, Grace most likely giving little Gracie instructions on how to take care of *him*.

Her lack of faith in him stung. Grace didn't think he could be responsible for himself, let alone Gracie.

And after all he'd done that morning.

He glared after Grace when she drove away. He'd show her—and his parents—that he wasn't the same irresponsible kid he used to be.

Aware that little Gracie still watched after Grace, Johnny left the porch and went to her side. Her morning's exuberance had waned and she raised her arms to him. Johnny held her close a moment, her damp tennis shoes leaving dew marks on his gym shorts, her small arms squeezing tight, leaving imprints around his neck and in his heart. He wasn't going to lose this child.

"Do you want to play with the kittens some more?" Johnny asked her.

"They're tired." Gracie laid her head on his shoulder.

Johnny rocked her for a moment, gazing about the farm, his mood mellowing with the sense that here, time had stood still. The bottom porch step still had a squeak, the gravel lane had the same ruts and the yard still had the bare spot under the tree where Grace's tire swing—the one she wanted rehung—had been. The wagon wheel propped by the barn, bright daisies sprouting around it, had been there too.

Johnny caught a glimpse of green inside the open barn door. His ambling thoughts skidded to a halt.

The Greens' old Ford pickup. A vintage set of wheels even before the Greens had bought it.

Hadn't Grace said she wished it still ran, that first day he was in town?

Johnny wavered, the truck beckoning him to the barn, the syrupy silverware and scorched pan waiting for him at the house.

Do the responsible thing.

Johnny jiggled Gracie and whispered, "Hey, Snow White, I think I just found you a chariot."

And over the next few days little Gracie kept

Johnny's repairs a secret until finally, on Friday, she and Johnny drove the Greens' old pickup into town to surprise Grace.

Grace felt more attuned to the sun shining outside the wide salon window than to the task of pulling strands of Mrs. Cromwell's short graying hair through a plastic bonnet in preparation for freshening the florist's highlights. Grace had that go-to-the-park feeling again, dressed as she was in striped shorts, white shirt and leather sandals. At this moment, Johnny was probably at home giving Gracie a push on the old tire swing he'd tied to the elm with fresh rope.

Hanging that swing seemed Johnny's greatest accomplishment of the week. He hadn't gotten much done in the way of arranging his office, and Grace had come home more often than not to dirty dishes and to a tired, amazingly grimy little girl. In a way, Grace felt relieved. Johnny was keeping a close eye on Gracie.

In another way, she felt annoyed.

"Grace, dear, doesn't that old truck look familiar?" Mrs. Cromwell half rose from the chair to peer out the window, her ample body resplendent in a dress of her trademark flowers.

Grace turned to look beyond two customers who were sitting under the hoods of the hair dryers lined before the polished window. The sight of the old green Ford jerking to a halt at the curb had her heart turning. "That's daddy's truck."

Johnny climbed out from behind the wheel, then turned to lift Gracie out. Grace was still gazing at her father's old pickup when Johnny entered the shop, ushering little Gracie before him.

Mrs. Cromwell murmured, "Well, well. Johnny Tremont."

Ida Mayberry and Agatha Olsen, their white hair wrapped in pink curlers, swiveled beneath their dryer hoods to look at Johnny and little Gracie, drawing Grace's attention toward the door.

She caught her lip. Johnny and Gracie had apparently dressed for the occasion. Johnny's hair was still wet from his shower, and he was wearing what Grace was certain he considered his best shirt: a Harley-Davidson T-shirt, neatly tucked into his faded Levi's. Little Gracie, ducking behind Johnny to hide from the smiles she elicited, was wearing her ruffled blue pinafore and her pink tennis shoes.

Johnny grinned his sexy unabashed grin, undaunted by the stares he attracted from the elderly clientele, all of whom, Grace was certain, remembered him less than fondly. Marcy sauntered over from her station to stand beside Grace, a dubious surrogate mother in her tight denim skirt and hiking boots, her short bleached hair teased to stand on end.

Apparently sensing Grace was ill at ease, Mrs. Cromwell spoke above the hum of hair dryers. "Go say hello to your *husband,* dear. Marcy will tend to my highlights, won't you, Marcy?"

"Sure I will." But Marcy eyed Johnny suspiciously as Grace crossed to the door.

Grace knelt before Gracie, drawing her from behind Johnny's leg with a smile. "I like my surprise."

"Johnny said I could wear my wedding dress
when we brought the truck to town."

"You look very pretty." Right down to the frilly
white socks she wore with her scuffed play shoes.
"Why don't you go pick out a ribbon or barrette
from the drawer?"

Gracie wavered a moment, weighing her desire for
a hair bow against the prospect of walking before all
the ladies to get to the cash register. Ida was smiling,
Agatha dozing. Marcy winked at her and Mrs. Cromwell beamed. Gracie started slowly over.

Grace rose, wondering how to express her grate-
fulness to Johnny. Then she noticed he was staring
at Mrs. Cromwell, with her tufts of hair sticking out
the holes of the bonnet, as if the woman was an alien.
Mrs. Cromwell was staring back, probably still trying
to account for those sacks of fertilizer that had disappeared from her greenhouse every Halloween during the period of Johnny's residence in Ashville.

Little Gracie returned with a white bow and Grace
hastily fastened it in her hair, steering Johnny outside
on the pretext of looking at the truck. Johnny lifted
Gracie to play in the bed of the truck, then leaned
against it, arms crossed, looking pleased with himself.

Grace smiled, feeling suddenly as self-conscious
as she knew Gracie had been. She ran her hand along
the top of the truck bed, leaning to look inside the
open window. Besides getting the truck running,

Johnny had cleaned it up inside. The vinyl seats were dust-free, as was the dash with its big speedometer dial and no radio. The Greens had made their own music. Grace remembered falling asleep as a girl on the way home from the grocery store to their lullabies of Elvis ballads.

Her eyes burned over the thoughtfulness of Johnny's deed. No wonder little Gracie had been so grimy, and dirty dishes had been left in the sink.

"Hey, don't cry." Johnny moved closer, a touch of panic in his voice. Grace swiped at her brimming eyes, aware of Mrs. Cromwell watching intently out the window before Marcy sat her down and stuck a hair dryer over her head. "This was supposed to make you happy."

Grace watched little Gracie stomp about in the bed of the truck the way she used to do as a child. "I should have gotten rid of this thing a long time ago."

"Are you kidding? This old Ford is an antique." Johnny sounded appalled now, as much for his own sake as hers, Grace thought dryly.

But while his appreciation of the truck was practical, hers was purely sentimental. She sighed with pleasure. "I never was able to part with that truck—or get it running. Thank you, Johnny."

"You're welcome." His voice was deep and his eyes were warm as the summer sky. Sunlight burnished his hair and laid a golden haze over the quiet street. Grace could smell fresh wax on the gleaming pickup; she could hear little Gracie singing as she circled its bed. A shimmering awareness of the rightness of the moment came over Grace. If only time could stand still.

Marcy poked her head outside the salon door. "Ida Mayberry is dry."

Time marched on. Grace sighed. "Be right there."

Johnny beckoned little Gracie to the side of the truck. "Tell Grace the rest of our surprise."

"Johnny said we can have chicken-in-a-box at the park."

"A picnic?" Grace felt as delighted as little Gracie sounded. She'd been longing for a picnic at the park. But that meant Johnny and Gracie would have to wait in the salon while she finished her appointments.

That was a long time for Johnny to behave.

Still, Grace led them back inside. Johnny settled himself obediently in a chair near Grace's station, little Gracie on his lap, the two of them sharing a magazine. Grace combed out Ida Mayberry's hair, while Marcy combed out Agatha's. That left only Mrs. Cromwell in the salon, sitting beneath the hair dryer, a surprisingly kind expression on her face for Johnny.

The salon door opened. Grace silently groaned. She'd forgotten the appointment she'd made for William. She'd never get to the park.

"I can finish Mrs. Cromwell," Marcy offered.

"Would you? Johnny and Gracie have a picnic planned."

Johnny stopped reading to grimace at William, who was closing the door. Marcy grinned. "You bet

I will. Go ahead and give William his shampoo and trim.''

''Thanks, Marcy.''

''Well, if it isn't the newlyweds.'' Adjusting the tie he wore with a striped shirt, William walked over to Grace and, to her astonishment, placed his congratulatory kiss right on her mouth. He cocked his head at Johnny, and smiled down at little Gracie. Johnny and Gracie frowned up at him.

Grace forgot William's kiss, struck by the two sets of blue eyes glaring from beneath dark lashes, not only because of the resemblance she saw there, but because of the strength of the bond Johnny and Gracie seemed to share. Their mutual dislike for William was on their faces.

''Well, if it isn't Bill,'' Johnny replied.

Recalling the tense moments at the Dairy Dip, Grace flashed Johnny a warning look, but he only raised his brows innocently. She marched over to the sink and spun the chair around. ''I'm ready for you, William.''

Johnny and Gracie went back to their reading, though Grace didn't miss the disdain on Johnny's face when she tied the protective pink apron over William's starched shirt.

As she wet William's hair and massaged in shampoo, Grace tried to ignore Johnny. But she couldn't help noticing that William's pale hair wasn't as thick as Johnny's. It wasn't as shiny even when wet, wasn't nearly as soft as she remembered Johnny's to be that day at the farm when he'd kissed her—

"Ow! That water's hot!" William leaned away from the spray.

"Sorry." Grace hastily turned off the spray, appalled over the direction her thoughts had wandered. She heard Johnny snicker, and hoped Bill—*William*—hadn't heard.

"No problem." William followed her to her station and Grace set about trimming his hair, only half listening to his law tales, unable to understand how he could enjoy handling divorce cases with their heartbreaking custody battles.

Sitting in Marcy's chair, Mrs. Cromwell seemed to feel the same. "I would think you'd strive harder to reunite those families that have children, William," she scolded.

"Marriage isn't always in the best interest of the child," William replied, and Grace stilled, her gaze darting to Johnny's. Had she only imagined William's innuendo? Johnny appeared as tense as she felt, winding his arm protectively around little Gracie. Gracie snuggled closer to him, turning a page of their magazine. Grace spun William in the chair, away from the threat that darkened Johnny's gaze.

She and Johnny were overreacting, expecting someone to figure out the true purpose of their hasty marriage.

Grace forced herself to stay calm and resumed work, leaning to lift sections of William's hair, trimming off some, then letting the strands slip through her fingers. She was aware of Johnny watching intently, probably unable to shake off William's innocent comment. She thought how she would enjoy shampooing and trimming Johnny's thick dark hair, enjoy having her hands in *his* hair this way.

The screech of chair legs on the linoleum floor had Grace gritting her teeth and nearly leaving William with a bald spot on the side of his head. It was Johnny, of course.

"I need some fresh air," he growled, setting Gracie on her feet. He stood, as tensely wound as a too-tight perm, his animosity toward William poorly disguised. Grace thought it didn't help when, this time, Marcy snickered.

"I like this air," Gracie said, and Grace was certain the little girl was reminded of times her mother had taken her along to the salon.

"Gracie can stay with me if she likes." She hoped little Gracie would stay. Johnny needed a moment to unwind.

"I'll be right out on the sidewalk," he told Gracie reassuringly. And Gracie settled contentedly in her chair, now and then waving to him through the window.

Grace finished William's haircut in record time, relieved when he walked out the door. From the window she saw that Johnny was leaning against the truck, waiting for her and Gracie. She went over to the little girl, and knelt to tie Gracie's shoe. "Why don't you go use the ladies' room and wash your hands," she suggested. "Then we can have our picnic."

Gracie readily complied. Grace collected Mrs.

Cromwell's payment for Marcy, and bade her good-bye as the woman waddled out the door, patting her highlighted hair.

A moment later, she bustled back in, her flowered skirt flapping, her purse clutched to her bosom, her eyes big as the blossoms on her dress. "Grace, dear! The men are having a fight!"

Grace glanced out the window in time to see Johnny's fist connect with William's face.

Chapter Seven

"Y ouch!" Johnny abandoned all pretense of stoicism as Grace held his hand over a salon sink and doused his skinned knuckles with peroxide.

The pain failed to divert him from an astonishing replay in his mind of Mrs. Cromwell sending William off like a naughty boy caught filching flowers. The way, Johnny recalled, she used to send *him* home from the greenhouse.

For a while today, Johnny had been certain Mrs. Cromwell had figured out the Halloween mystery of the disappearing fertilizer bags. Instead, he'd somehow wound up in her good graces, probably because she'd seen William strike the first blow. But he strongly suspected she'd overheard William refuse to take back a sly comment on the obvious side benefit of his convenient marriage to Grace.

"Youch!"

Grace, however, was mad at him.

"Youch!"

Real mad. There was no sympathy coming from her direction, despite the fact that Mrs. Cromwell had assured her he'd only been defending himself. Her gaze stung like the peroxide she burned the hide off his hand with. He supposed he ought to be sorry for taking a punch at one of her customers right outside of her shop, but it had practically been a reflex action after Bill sucker-punched him. And when he thought of what Bill had said, he wasn't sorry at all.

"Really, Johnny." Grace distracted him from his anger with her disgust as she inspected his hand. While Johnny hoped she thought the scrapes were clean, he wasn't about to argue with her decision. "What were you thinking of, scuffling in the street like a schoolboy?"

At least Grace was unaware of what Bill had said. She had enough to worry about in their battle to keep Gracie. And Johnny knew he'd done nothing to ease that worry, his behavior today hardly the kind to enhance his image as a responsible guardian for Gracie.

Though it had felt pretty good at the time.

"Did you *fall again,* Johnny?" Gracie pressed against his leg, peering over the sink, her big worried eyes making him grateful she hadn't witnessed the fight. Not that it really counted as a fight. Bill had been more than happy to heed Mrs. Cromwell's invitation to leave.

"I didn't fall," Johnny reassured Gracie. "I just—

ah—did something kind of dumb and skinned up my hand.''

"I think this needs a bandage," Grace said, indicating his index finger.

Johnny normally would have scoffed at that, the way he'd wanted to scoff at the peroxide. But little Gracie jumped at the chance to play nurse and Grace was already angry enough, so he meekly allowed Grace and little Gracie to each bandage a finger. Gracie's was so loose it wouldn't last long anyway, while Grace's was tight enough that he suspected she envisioned it around his neck.

It didn't help that Grace's mother hen, Marcy, stood smirking at him. She obviously enjoyed watching him grovel. Johnny eyed the woman back. Grace had told him a little about her, how Marcy had come to town a year ago, a divorced city girl looking to make a home for her daughter. She and Grace were of the same age and it was clear they had become friends as well as co-workers. Johnny thought Marcy's dark eyes reflected a woman whose past was as flawed as his. She and Grace seemed an odd pairing. Strangely, that thought seemed to mellow him toward her. "How about joining us for lunch, Marcy? My treat."

That ought to soothe Grace's ruffled feathers a bit, Johnny thought smugly. But Marcy seemed unimpressed, and remained silent.

Grace loved the idea. "You could pick up Mindy from day care. She and Gracie can play together at the park."

Marcy hesitated, just long enough to let Johnny know she wasn't that easy. He'd already decided it was going to take more than a box of chicken to win her over.

"I'll go get Mindy," Marcy finally said.

"We'll meet you at the park," Grace told her.

Johnny left the women to gather their purses while he took Gracie out to the truck. Gracie was kissing his injured hand to make it better when Grace joined them. He caught Grace's reluctant smile and entertained the notion that another kiss might be forthcoming. But Grace immediately engaged little Gracie in conversation, leaving Johnny to drive to the edge of town for chicken, then back to the center of town to Ashville Park where they met up with Marcy and her daughter.

Marcy's daughter, Mindy, was a rambunctious contrast to Gracie, who hung back shyly over lunch. But the ride Johnny gave them on the merry-go-round jump-started a round of giggles from both dizzy little girls.

They went off with Grace and Marcy to feed leftover biscuits to the ducks in the pond, while Johnny dropped down on the blanket he'd spread over shade-cooled grass beneath the far-reaching limbs of an oak. He lay back and closed his eyes. He was glad little Gracie had made a friend who would start school with her this fall. It would be nice to see Gracie and Mindy's friendship grow over the years the way Grace and Janelle's had, with him and Grace bringing the girls to the park or taking them to the movies—

Only he and Grace wouldn't still be married over the years.

Soft swishing steps sounded in the grass. Johnny felt a tug on the blanket, and caught Grace's subtle sweet scent as she sat beside him. He could feel her watching him, but his mind kept revolving around thoughts of the past. And the future…

"You're awfully quiet," Grace noted after a while.

Johnny opened his eyes and shook off the melancholy mood that had claimed him. "I was just…thinking about Janelle."

"Me too," she said softly.

Johnny sat up. "I won't get in any more fights," he promised her. "I won't risk losing Gracie."

"Should I even ask what that fight was about?"

Johnny pressed his lips together firmly. He wasn't about to repeat Bill's innuendo to Grace.

"Never mind." Grace sighed. "William does kind of grate on one's nerves at times—not that he'll likely be back to the salon to grate on mine," she added dryly.

Johnny grinned. Grace never could stay mad at him for long. And he was glad Bill wouldn't be back, and wouldn't be kissing Grace again.

The breeze laced Grace's silky hair across her sun-grazed cheeks. Johnny followed her movements as she caught the wayward strands with her slim fingers and brushed them behind her ear. She lounged back on her hands and stretched out her legs, which were long and lithe below her sexy striped shorts. When she crossed one sandal-clad foot over the other, Johnny silently suffered a wave of unfulfilled desire. Keeping his focus above her collar only made him achingly aware of her lips. And her lips made him want to kiss her...

"Grace." Marcy came marching over—it was the only word to describe her stride in those army boots she wore. Johnny suspected she'd noticed things were getting too cozy here on the blanket. "Gracie wants you to give them a push on the swings."

Johnny noticed Grace hesitate, despite her obvious pleasure over little Gracie's request. She seemed very careful about acting more like a friend than a parent to Gracie, knowing it was a role she could continue once they were divorced. He ought to appreciate that, he knew. Somehow, he didn't.

Probably because of Marcy, Johnny decided, looking up at her frowning face. That distrustful look of hers made a guy feel as if he'd stolen his Grandma's Harley.

Grace rose, and Johnny suffered the torment of viewing her long lithe legs from a fresh angle. He felt Marcy's suspicious gaze once more and averted his own.

Grace's desire to play with the girls had apparently won out over her caution. "I think I'll take the girls down the slide, too."

Grace walked off. Johnny had never realized how much he liked striped shorts. Suddenly he was looking at a swatch of denim, the sturdy legs below leading to hiking boots. Johnny sighed. "Have a seat, Marcy."

"I was thinking more along the lines of having a talk."

Women always wanted to talk. Maybe that was what he'd always liked about Grace. He could hang around her and not get his ear talked off. When they did talk, it was always about something interesting, like who'd painted what on the town water tower. Johnny pushed himself to his feet. He didn't think that was going to be the case with Marcy.

He figured he'd wait for Marcy to start the conversation, since she was the one with something to say.

He didn't have to wait long.

"Grace tells me you knew each other as teens."

"Yeah, we did." With effort, Johnny kept from sounding too defensive. He knew where this conversation was heading. He hadn't missed Marcy's protective air where Grace was concerned. Though he knew he should like her for it, thus far her attitude only irritated him.

"She said you moved here from Chicago, then went back after you graduated."

"Yeah, I did." Johnny walked over to the picnic table where they'd sat for lunch and started stacking boxes to throw away. Marcy marched after him.

"So you were gone about ten years."

"Yeah."

"Funny, Grace never mentioned you." Leaning

across the table, Marcy jammed paper cups into the box he was holding. Johnny tightened his grip on the box to keep from dropping it.

"We kept in touch." It was what they'd decided to tell everyone, for in a sense it was true. Janelle had shared news from Grace's letters over the years, telling him of the Greens' deaths, of Grace going to school and starting her salon and trying to keep the farm. And Grace had learned about his cycle business, which was all there was to know about him. Johnny met Marcy's challenging gaze.

She braced her hands on the table. "I'd say you moved pretty fast when you came back to town."

His temper flared. He dropped the box on the table and lined up his hands with hers. "In case you didn't notice, I *married* Grace."

"Yeah," Marcy said gruffly. "And I figure you two had your reasons."

The way her gaze flickered to Gracie, it was apparent Marcy had her suspicions, the same as Bill had. Hell, all of Ashville probably knew by now that his parents were trying to take Gracie from him. The thought stirred every protective instinct he had for his niece. "And here I thought you were worried about Grace."

"I *am* worried about Grace." Marcy leaned closer, clearly unintimidated. "Did she tell you when I first came here, I was in danger of losing Mindy to my ex? Grace gave me a job. I was able to support my daughter, to keep her."

A reluctant respect for Marcy mixed with Johnny's

annoyance. Still, he didn't back off. If Marcy understood about Gracie, what was her problem?

"Grace helped me find a place to live, too. She let me and Mindy stay with her until we could move in."

That sounded like something Grace would do, Johnny thought, even as his impatience with Marcy grew.

"What I'm telling you is that Grace is a *good* person. She's different from you and me." Narrowing her eyes, her hands now fisted on the table, Marcy warned, "I don't want to see her get hurt."

Johnny let his breath flare out. "I would never hurt Grace."

"I've seen the way you look at her. I've seen the way *she* looks at you. She's innocent. You could take advantage of that."

"She's a grown woman," he shot back. They were face to face now over the table, knuckle to knuckle. "She knows her own mind."

"No," Marcy said more forcefully. "I mean she's *innocent.*"

Her meaning filtered through Johnny's mind past the hazy sound of the little girls playing, past the hushed voice of the breeze in his ears, past the drone of slow-moving traffic around the park square.

Innocent.

Grace was a virgin.

"Johnny! Marcy!" Hands on her hips, Grace called to them from near the slide. "Is everything all right?"

Johnny focused again and read the threat in Marcy's eyes. Though he would hardly consider filling Grace in on their conversation, he was too stunned to take offense. He stepped back from the table. "We're—ah—just cleaning up here."

Grace frowned, then started over.

Marcy grabbed plastic forks and dropped them in the box. In a low voice she told him, "One night when Grace had a cold, I made her a whiskey and honey. Grace is no drinker. That's when she told me."

"I didn't know," he said inanely, still shocked by the revelation.

"I'm relieved to hear that," Marcy said pointedly.

Johnny might have laughed at her audacity, but Marcy was serious and at that moment Grace walked up to join them.

Marcy shoved the box full of trash into Johnny's hands, then turned to Grace, "I've got to give a perm at one-thirty. I'd better get Mindy back to day care." She shot Johnny a loaded look and said sweetly, "I owe you."

"Don't give it another thought." Johnny shot the look right back.

As soon as Marcy was out of hearing range, Grace turned to him and demanded, "All right. What were you two fighting about?"

Maybe it was his imagination, but he swore he could *see* Grace's innocence now, like a glow of pureness about her. It was in her eyes as well, the depth of her inexperience revealed by a naiveté he hadn't noticed before.

So why was he the one who suddenly felt vulnerable? "We weren't fighting, we were just—ah—talking."

Grace let out her breath in a huff. "You can't be trusted alone for a moment."

She stalked after Marcy, leaving Johnny to hope that wasn't true.

Still stunned by Marcy's revelation, he watched Grace walk away. His wanting for her came over him in a lonely wave. He understood now why Marcy felt so protective of Grace. And he was more certain than ever that Grace deserved someone special in her life.

He wasn't going to hurt Grace, no matter what Marcy might think. He *cared* about Grace. He always had. Hadn't he fixed the chain on her bike? Driven her and Janelle to town to see the movies?

But what Marcy had said was true. Grace was different from them—from *him*. Once he was assured guardianship of Gracie, once the furor died down, he would ease himself and Gracie out of her house, to the fringes of her life, so that she could find some guy to give her heart to.

A guy who had a heart to give her in return.

"I'll have orange." Keeping one hand on the truck's steering wheel, Johnny accepted the lollipop little Gracie gave him. He knew the cherry one was Gracie's favorite flavor. Old Henry Gold had really come through today, giving Gracie two lollipops. He kind of liked to think Henry had intended for him to have one. He'd worked hard in the past week to prove how responsible he could be while Grace was at the salon. Unfortunately, the challenge had failed to keep his mind off his attraction to Grace.

He knew he ought to set up his office in the den as planned and try to distract himself with work. Though he rather liked mowing the lawn, playing with Gracie, even buying groceries. In Chicago, he'd mostly eaten out, or had carryout. He'd never realized you could buy those little square hamburgers frozen in a box. Grace wouldn't have to cook tonight.

Turning into the lane at the farm, Johnny slowed the truck and let little Gracie climb into his lap to steer the rest of the way to the house. He peered over top of the white bow she wore with her Snow White T-shirt as Gracie skirted a rut in the gravel. The kid was a natural.

When they stopped before the garage, Johnny gave Gracie a hug, then sat a moment while she pretended she was still driving. As he gazed at the closed garage door, his Harley behind it, work lost all appeal.

He propped his arm on the truck door and drummed his fingers against it. Gracie ought to have a bike, too. A bicycle. It seemed like more of a priority than setting up an office. The truth was, his business practically ran itself. He had a good crew in the garage, and any problems with sales he could handle by phone. Hell, if he went out of business today, he could live off his investments.

He contemplated the Greens' garage, recalling how he'd often come here to work on his Harley, Janelle and Grace hanging about to pester him. He suddenly felt as if he'd come full circle, back to Ashville. Only this time, he wanted to stay.

"Hey, Snow White." Johnny shifted Gracie sideways on his lap. "You want to see if Grace has a bike in the garage that you could ride?"

"A *real* bike?"

"Sure." As opposed to pretend? Johnny wondered.

"I'm too big for my tricycle," Gracie explained. That solemn look that always got to Johnny came into her eyes. He held her close. "Mommy and Daddy said they would get me a real bike for my birthday," she said.

"Oh, they did?" Ignoring the ache in his chest, Johnny raised his brows suggestively. "Now that I think of it, Grace and I still have to figure out something to get you."

"They were getting me a pink bike," Gracie added, just in case.

The prettiest, pinkest bike he could find.

"Think you can get by for a while on one of Grace's old bikes?" Grace's father had been a traditional farmer; he'd never thrown anything away. A kindred spirit, Johnny thought.

"Can we go in the garage?"

Johnny grinned. Gracie loved to play inside while he tinkered with the Harley. "I guess we'll just have to."

"We have to put away the groceries and eat our lunch first."

Typical woman. "Yes, we do."

"But we can wash dishes later," Gracie added.

She was learning.

Johnny really was trying, Grace thought as she perused the contents of the freezer. There were a few dishes in the sink, but he had apparently driven the truck—which was proving quite handy—into town for groceries.

Ice cream. Hot dogs. *Square* hamburgers?

She set out a package of chicken and closed the freezer door. Johnny and Gracie were nowhere in sight. She curved her lips wryly. At least she knew where to find them. She only hoped Johnny had had Gracie change out of her favorite Snow White shirt before they went out to the garage.

She left the kitchen, passing by the *still* unconverted den, and headed for the front door. If Johnny chose to run his business by cellular phone from her garage, that was his decision. But if he'd let another of Gracie's shirts be ruined, he was in for a lecture.

Once outside, Grace heard the roar of Johnny's Harley, the sound seeming to reverberate right through her. She stepped to the edge of the porch and gazed across the yard to where Johnny had moved the Harley outside the garage. He revved the engine repeatedly, and she felt the vibrations blend into one giant shiver. Most men likened the lure of the bike to a lust for power, while Johnny had always said the lure was freedom. She wondered how he saw it now, with little Gracie standing at his side.

Johnny was crouched beside the Harley, his broad back to her, his navy muscle shirt hanging loose of his jeans as he adjusted the carburetor, the way she'd seen him do it countless times. A wave of nostalgia swept over her, cresting at her heart. Grace felt all of fifteen again, living for the moment Johnny would notice her and grin.

The hot breeze blew his hair, whipped his shirt to his back, then billowed beneath it. In her tan shorts and cool gauzy shirt, Grace grew warm. She stepped into the sun and walked over.

Johnny rose, and it was all Grace could do not to falter. Sun rays glossed his hair and turned his tanned arms to copper. His eyes were as dark as his shirt, the desire in them reaching across the expanse of gravel and grass to stir her. The heat of the breeze licked at the backs of her legs while she watched him through the curtain of her hair, blown across her cheeks. Maybe Johnny's need wasn't as deep as hers, but it was magnetic, drawing her closer even as her heart beat a warning with each step she took.

"Grace, I'm helping!"

Little Gracie came running up, bringing yet another threat to Grace's heart. She longed to gather the child in her arms, but settled for straightening Gracie's white bow atop her hair, which was tangled by the summer wind. A layer of dust powdered Gracie's fine skin and her little hands were grimy. Then Grace noticed what Gracie was wearing: one of

Johnny's white T-shirts over her clothes, dragging about the soles of her tennis shoes.

"I'm staying clean." Gracie wiped her hands on Johnny's white shirt, apparently assured that Snow White was safe beneath it.

Grace wasn't so sure, though she didn't say so to Gracie, giving her a smile instead. But it helped to focus on Snow White's fate as opposed to her own. When Gracie ran back to Johnny, Grace met his sinful gaze sternly.

But Johnny only grinned at her, sending a fresh rush of heat through her body. He leaned down and whispered to Gracie, who then disappeared into the garage.

He sauntered her way, his navy shirt blown flat against his belly. He carried a screwdriver, tapping it against the palm of his free hand. The walk was vintage Johnny—cocky, sexy, and combined with his grin, devastating to a lovesick girl. Grace felt like that girl again now, her knees trembly, her stomach fluttering, her heart beating hard. The worst of it was that Johnny knew it; his gaze was full of masculine self-assurance.

They met toe to toe a few yards from the Harley. "I can see you've been busy," she said tartly.

Undaunted, Johnny replied, "Wait until you see what I did."

How many times had she heard that as a teen, only to discover that what Johnny had been so proud of was enough to put him on probation? Grace braced herself, but nothing could have prepared her for the

heart-melting sight of Gracie pedaling her old mini-
ature two-wheeler out of the garage. It was the bike
her parents had given her when she was five. It was
more rust than white now, but little Gracie didn't
seem to care, riding about in her shirt-dress in happy
abandon.

Until the bike's chain fell off.

"Uh-oh," Johnny said.

Jarred when the chain slipped, Gracie managed to
stay upright to stop the bike. But her smile vanished.
Her lip trembled. "Can you fix it, Johnny?"

Johnny was already walking over, reaching to
shove the screwdriver in his back jeans pocket, pushing his low-slung jeans even lower. His loose shirt
gathered above the screwdriver handle, revealing his
lean denim-clad hip. As he came to little Gracie's
rescue, patiently fixing the bike chain the way he'd
fixed Grace's bike as a teen, Grace fought a flaming
desire all the more potent for the tenderness that
swamped her. In contrast, Johnny appeared amazingly content, as if repairing her old bike was as fulfilling as cleaning the carburetor on a five-figure Harley.

But then, beneath Johnny's bad-boy exterior,
hadn't there always been a goodness, a kindness inside that had drawn her to him? Somehow, those
traits seemed more compelling now that he was a
man. Johnny was nothing short of irresistible as he
knelt beside Gracie, who rested her hand on his
shoulder while he worked the chain back over the
sprocket, showing her how as he did.

Sunlight pooled around Gracie and Johnny, bathing them in gold and creating the appearance of an aged photograph she might have been looking back on years from now.

She fought a welling of emotion for Gracie and Johnny, vowing again to be careful with Gracie's feelings, and achingly aware Johnny suffered no such turmoil over her. The Tremonts posed a real threat in regard to guardianship of little Gracie. They telephoned her on a regular basis and Gracie was excited about the trip to the Oceanarium in Chicago they had promised for her upcoming birthday. If Gracie had to return to Chicago to live with the Tremonts, she knew Johnny would go, too.

In that moment, she wished that Johnny had never come back. In the next, she wanted desperately for him to stay.

"All set." His hand on his knee, Johnny levered himself up while Gracie set off once more on her gleeful circling. Johnny wondered how she didn't get dizzy. And he wondered how Grace could stand there in the midst of the heat and the dust and the tension and not break a sweat. He was burning, inside and out, while she gazed at him, coolly affronted by God knew what.

Hadn't he made certain Gracie kept clean? He'd gone to town for groceries, been respectful to old Henry Gold. Hell, he'd even waved to Bill, though the guy had seemed in kind of a hurry. And he knew she was pleased about the bike, for he'd seen the glow in her eyes at the sight of Gracie riding it.

He gazed back at Grace. Her green eyes reminded him of sunlight shimmering on the still pond in the Greens' back pasture. There was more going on beneath the surface than she intended for him to see. He hadn't imagined her response when he'd approached her moments ago—that irresistible combination of heated awareness and innocent longing. He felt it again now, tenfold.

The moment simmered between them until finally Grace murmured something about supper and walked toward the house.

Johnny curled his hands. She wanted him. As surely as he wanted her.

But the idea of being her first both overwhelmed and awed him. The responsibility. The honor. To have such an important role in Grace's life...

He drew a stabilizing breath. His role in her life was *temporary*. Grace would only be sorry if they acted on impulse. Her first time should be special, with a man capable of love, a man she could love in return.

That certainly left him out. Grace knew him too well—all the faults he had, all the trouble he'd caused. All the trouble he was capable of causing...

She deserved the best kind of guy: white-collar, respectable, no reputation as a juvenile delinquent. Someone like a banker, or a doctor, or a lawyer...like Bill—

Johnny winced. He'd better be careful, or he'd convince himself he was saving Grace.

* * *

In the days to come, the weather grew oppressive, still and hot, as did Johnny's desire for Grace.

It didn't help that they kept Gracie mainly in the air-conditioned house, the confinement only adding to his awareness of Grace. When temperatures cooled the following Sunday, they spent the day fishing and wading in the Greens' pond. But that didn't help either, for Grace wore shorts and a halter shirt that skimmed above and below her breasts and quite simply drove him crazy. That night, Johnny thought he was more tormented by Grace's sunburn than she, as he lay on his pallet of blankets and listened to her soft moans, imagining the tan lines on her creamy skin.

It was a relief to head into town the next day to sign up Gracie for kindergarten. He couldn't have stood another day of Grace wading the pond in her little shorts and shirt.

Ashville School, near the north edge of town, appeared unchanged to Johnny, with the exception that the trees outside were taller and the building looked somehow smaller. All twelve grades were taught here, and volunteers were taking the grade school kids for a tour through the elementary wing while parents contended with the paperwork.

Johnny followed Grace and little Gracie inside the school, grateful Grace's pretty apricot flowered dress reached past her knees. But she'd worn her sandals again and Johnny tripped going up the short set of stairs, his gaze on Grace's slender ankles.

He heard a familiar snicker of disdain, recognized

the distinctive cadence of steps behind him. He turned. Marcy wore a flowered dress, too, in hot pink, and her outfit was accented by her hiking boots. Somehow, with her punk hairdo, she managed to make a successful fashion statement. It wasn't the only statement she had to make, of course.

"Well, if it isn't the Tremonts." Marcy grinned at Grace and smirked at Johnny as she got in line behind them to register Mindy for school. Johnny smirked back, but he winked at the little blond replica of Marcy standing at her side. Mindy winked, too, then turned to whisper to Gracie, who, after a shy start, was soon whispering back to her friend.

"I'm going to go sign up as a classroom chaperon," Marcy announced.

Johnny wondered how many parents would be willing to trust the care of their child on a field trip to Marcy, who generally looked as though she was on her way to a rock concert. Oddly, he realized *he* would.

"Would you sign us up, too?" Grace asked, and Johnny felt complimented that she would assume he was field trip material. He vaguely recalled being banned from the majority of those trips as a kid.

Marcy raised her brows consideringly at Johnny, apparently harboring reciprocal doubts over him. But she must have decided she'd trust him with her kid, too, for all she said was, "Consider it done."

"We'll save your place in line," Johnny offered magnanimously.

Promising Gracie they'd be right back, Marcy and

Mindy left. Johnny was aware of little Gracie clutching his leg as she watched the signing and shuffling of papers at the table ahead. Mostly she stared at the stern-faced woman with gray hair and horn-rimmed glasses who handed out the papers, gathered them up, then aligned them with a rap on the tabletop before filing them in the appropriate box. With a Volunteer's badge pinned over her left breast, the woman reminded Johnny of teachers he'd had who would have better served society in the military. Unconsciously, he wrapped a protective arm around little Gracie.

Grace seemed to notice Gracie's reaction, as well, for she caught Gracie's hand reassuringly, inching closer to Gracie and him.

Johnny looked down on Grace's silky hair, neatly parted and shiny. Her cheeks were pink from the sun, and her body looked slim and firm in her swingy dress. She appeared as fresh and young as the teenage girls signing up for high school. His frustration simmered with the knowledge that Grace was more innocent than some of those girls as she waited for the right man to come into her life. Considering little Gracie, Johnny couldn't help but believe that was how it should be for all young girls.

Still, he couldn't help wondering how he'd never come to steal a kiss from Grace her first year in high school—and his last. She'd always been a pretty girl. Of course, back then, he hadn't chosen who he kissed by the color of their eyes. Grace certainly met all the requirements now.

The austere voice of the woman in horn-rims pulled Johnny unwillingly from his thoughts.

"Young lady, go along with that group leaving to tour the elementary classrooms."

Little Gracie was definitely clinging now, and squeezing Grace's hand until her small knuckles were white.

"She's going to wait for her friend, Mindy, to go with her," Johnny informed the woman, earning a frown.

"If you want her to have her tour while you sign up, she must leave *now*."

"She doesn't want to go *now*," Johnny reiterated, with a rush of defiance worthy of a fifteen-year-old.

The woman glared at him over top of her glasses. Johnny glared back. Grace caught her lip, remembering similar standoffs in Johnny's past. He'd never been fazed by authority—and certainly not by a school volunteer.

But this time seemed different. Johnny was standing up for little Gracie against a woman who obviously had a control complex. Grace's apprehension evaporated, and she silently cheered him on.

The standoff ended abruptly, however, with the return of Marcy and Mindy. With a little coaxing, Gracie walked off hand in hand with Mindy. Grace felt a measure of relief that Gracie had taken this step toward school with her friend. Gracie still rarely let Johnny out of her sight, and that didn't bode well for the start of school. She couldn't bear to think how little Gracie would react if she had to leave Johnny to go live with the Tremonts.

Grace noticed then that Johnny stood staring after Gracie, the look on his face making her worry how *he* was going to handle Gracie's first day of school. He suddenly ushered her toward an empty corridor. "Let's take a stroll down memory lane."

"But I don't think we're supposed to—" She didn't bother to finish her sentence. Johnny had never been one to worry about what he was not supposed to do. She called back to Marcy, "Are you coming along?"

Poised to sign up Mindy for school, Marcy hesitated, then shook her head in answer. But she watched after them as Johnny ignored yet another glare from the volunteer to steer Grace down the deserted hall.

With the exuberance of a child, Johnny peered into unlocked classrooms, exclaiming over what had changed and what had remained the same. Grace marveled over the detail of his memories; she hadn't thought he'd paid that much attention to anything in school, except perhaps the girls.

School had been different for Johnny than for her. After he had graduated and left, her mother's illness had progressed, leaving little chance to socialize. Janelle had been there for her through those rough times, but Grace had pined after Johnny with each piece of her broken heart.

Then Janelle had gone off to college and met Grant, and Grace had attended a local school of cosmetology. There had been no time to seriously date a man or consider marriage. No time at all.

"Look, the hole is still in the ceiling."

Johnny took her hand and pulled her into the science lab. The damage he'd done with the hydrogen generator was still evident. But even as she gazed upward, Grace's attention was focused on the rough warmth of Johnny's hand wrapped securely around hers.

"My locker was just up the hall." Johnny pulled her out of the room and along the hall. Grace let herself be led, wondering how many hours she'd spent imagining herself walking hand in hand through school with Johnny.

He stopped, let go of her hand, opened his locker and poked his head inside. "This brings back memories. Whoever had this locker stuck his used gum in the same place."

Grace wrinkled her nose at that. But when Johnny stepped back, she peeked inside. It looked like all the other lockers, with the exception of the phone numbers scratched on the inside of the door. The initials *L.L.* were carved beside one set of digits.

L.L. Lorraine Lawson. Disgusted, Grace straightened.

Johnny must have noticed her pique because he shut the locker door with a quick smile. "Good old Lorraine. Shall we, ah, go check out your locker?"

"I think we'd better get back before Gracie does." Besides, there weren't any phone numbers scratched into her locker door to read.

Johnny went along peacefully until they came to Grace's locker. He leaned beside it, grinning, his hands shoved in his front jeans pockets. Wearing a gray Chicago Cubs baseball shirt, he looked like the jock he'd never been. He'd always been too busy with his motorcycles to play sports—or to do much of anything else. Thinking of her unconverted den, Grace grimaced. Johnny was *still* too busy with his motorcycles.

"Bet you never stuck used gum in the top of your locker," Johnny said shrewdly. "Or wrote your phone number on some guy's locker door."

"How do you know?" He surely hadn't paid any attention to her as a freshman. He'd been too busy plotting to leave town after his graduation.

"Because you were one of the 'good girls.'"

"That sounds like a classification." One she was sure hadn't held favor with the boys.

"There were two kinds of girls," Johnny explained, apparently warming to his subject. "The kind you took on the back seat of your car—"

Despite herself, Grace had to smother a laugh.

"And the kind you took to the prom," he finished on a more demure note.

"I never went to the prom," Grace informed him, then wished she hadn't reminded him of her lack of sophistication back then.

"You were one of the good girls," Johnny repeated, and Grace wondered over the certainty in his voice. Johnny couldn't have known *that* about her. But when his gaze softened, she felt as if he knew, and understood, everything about her. "It was never easy for you with your mother so ill."

Grace didn't want Johnny feeling sorry for her. If all she'd had was his friendship, she didn't want to think it had been based on pity. "You made her feel happy lots of times when you came to visit."

"That's just because she thought I looked like Elvis."

"Did she?" Grace leaned against her locker door. He'd never told her that.

"Yeah. I guess sometimes she was just confused, but I like to think she really saw a resemblance."

He curled his lip and ran a hand through his hair in imitation of Elvis. Grace laughed, but the good warm feeling inside her came from the kindness Johnny had shown her mother.

"I think you must be one of the good *guys,*" Grace told him.

"I didn't go to the prom either," he reminded her. Suddenly sober he added, "I wasn't good at all. But I'd have taken you to the prom if I'd still been here and you wanted to go."

"Only if Janelle made you," she said dryly, though her heartbeat quickened with his words. With Johnny gone, she'd never cared about going to the prom. But countless times she imagined that he'd never left, that they'd danced at the prom to something slow and romantic, sung by Elvis.

"Maybe I'd have *wanted* to take you to the prom," Johnny teased, moving in on her until her back was to the cool metal locker. "Maybe I'd have wanted to take you on the back seat of my... Harley.''

He was being facetious, of course. But Johnny's voice had grown huskier with each word he spoke. He'd braced his hands at either side of her face and Grace felt the heat of his body. His nearness filled her with longing. *If only...*

She struggled to hide the need that rose inside her. She could feel the tension emanate from Johnny, could see it in his riveting gaze. She knew his desire stemmed from his recent denial of the sexual aspects of his life. She knew she couldn't let him kiss her—

He kissed her.

Full and hot on her lips. An endless searing kiss that tasted of Johnny's frustration, his impatience, and beneath it all, his kindness. Whiskey laced with honey.

Overwhelmed, Grace kissed him back.

In that instant her frustration equaled his. She ached for Johnny to touch her, his body a scant inch from hers, the warmth of him seeming to seep right through her dress, her skin. She flattened her palms against the locker, some distant protective instinct holding her back from the embrace she yearned for. But as the sweetness of Johnny's kiss deepened, she could almost believe that he'd changed, that he might actually have come to care for her. Caution crumbled, and Grace raised her hands to his waist to draw Johnny closer.

''A-hem.'' The clearing of a throat broke the kiss

in a way the click of leather wing tips on the linoleum floor had failed to do.

It was Mr. Norton, principal of Ashville School for as long as Grace could remember. Grace hastily lowered her hands while Johnny drew away more slowly. With hope sparking within her from Johnny's kiss, Grace thought the tension pulsing between them had to be visible. She knew her cheeks were burning. Even Johnny seemed ruffled by the intrusion, shoving his hands in his pockets and remaining uncharacteristically quiet in the presence of the principal he'd once driven to distraction.

Mr. Norton's hair, which coincidentally had started graying during Johnny's first year in attendance, was the same thick stark white it had been at Johnny's graduation. He still wore the suspicious look he'd adopted back then, an effect Johnny had seemed to have on the whole school administration.

The principal's gaze flickered between them, settling on Johnny, most likely out of old habit.

"Mr. Tremont. It seems like old times." Mr. Norton made his point dryly.

Old times. With those words, Grace's belief that Johnny might feel something for *her* faded once more to an unfulfilled wish. Johnny had likely stolen numerous kisses in these school halls, had undoubtedly been swept up by a sense of nostalgia today. His answering comment only seemed to confirm that likelihood.

"I guess I got caught up in the past," he murmured, and Grace felt the last embers of hope within her burn out.

Mr. Norton turned to her then. "Grace, Mrs. Norton and I missed seeing you at the past couple of Sunday services. The reverend told us of your marriage to Johnny."

"We've been busy, but we hope to attend soon." Grace scarcely noticed when Johnny only dipped his head in agreement, a numbness creeping over her. She'd known better.

Voices drifted down the hall. Their trip around the school had brought them back near the front hall. As Mr. Norton offered his congratulations on their recent marriage and welcomed Gracie to the school system, Grace thought how, before long, her and Johnny's divorce would be the talk of the town. Everyone would understand then that they had done it for little Gracie. Just as she understood.

Mr. Norton continued down the corridor and Grace moved toward the front hall. Johnny walked along without comment, seeming deep in thought, apparently as aware of their transgression as she.

Little Gracie and Mindy had returned, with Marcy there to greet them. Gracie held up a gold star, her name printed in childish scrawl upon it. Grace fought the yearning to rush over and praise Gracie's accomplishment, and instead kept her steps measured. But the sound of a female voice purring Johnny's name brought her to a complete halt.

"*Johnny*. I heard you were back in town." The brunette that came with the voice was catlike thin and intent on wrapping her arms around him. She found his mouth unerringly with her bright red lips, giving a dramatic kiss that had Grace recalling the brunette's part in a high school play. She left no doubt that she had kissed Johnny before.

"Nice to see you…ah—"

Vanessa, she remembered, but Grace opted against helping Johnny in his obvious struggle to place a name to the face still close to his. There was no doubt in her mind that this meeting would end with Vanessa's name, address and phone number slipped into his pocket.

"Tell me I heard wrong, that you're not *married,*" the brunette went on in a voice heavy with theatrics. She swept Grace with a condescending glance that made her feel as if she hadn't changed at all from the awkward teen she'd once been.

"Grace and I—"

"My little boy is here…somewhere." The brunette gave a vague wave of her hand, and kept her attention, along with her other hand, on Johnny. "This is like old times. You've probably heard I'm divorced.…"

Grace, at least, had heard enough.

"Go ahead and visit," she told Johnny. "I'll wait outside with Gracie."

Some things never change, Grace thought, struggling not to stomp out of the school. Catching her reflection in a window, she reminded herself that she looked just fine, if not sexy like Vanessa. But there was no escaping the fact that Johnny was better

suited to the Vanessas and Lorraines of this world.
Women who didn't seek the kind of meaningful re-
lationship Johnny had never learned to believe in.
Never would…

Johnny watched Grace walk out of the school, and
wanted to shake the brunette off his arm and follow.

The intensity of that feeling staggered him. He'd
steamed up a lot of windows in his day, with a lot
of different women. But now the desire he felt was
specific, when it had never been before. He wanted
Grace.

Only Grace.

Outside, in the sparkle of sun, with the softness of
summer green all around them, he saw Grace kneel
before little Gracie. Caught up in the picture they
made, he scarcely noticed when the brunette abandoned her flirtation. As Grace bestowed a smile upon
little Gracie, his need for Grace meshed with the
burning desire he carried within him.

Then he caught Marcy's wary frown. Resentment
flared within him. He'd *changed.*

But there was a difference between being field trip
material and marriage material. Reminded that he
wasn't the kind of guy Grace waited for, the kind
she deserved, Johnny swallowed his resentment and
walked outside.

Chapter Eight

Grace heard a stirring in the night, small shuffling steps crossing the hall, stopping at the threshold of her bedroom. There was a small night lamp in the hall, but only faint moonlight to illuminate little Gracie's path in the bedroom. Accustomed now to Johnny "falling out of bed" and sleeping on the floor, Gracie unerringly crawled over him to climb into the bed with Grace.

Grace held little Gracie close as they leaned back on the pillows. She'd taken a few days off from work to spend with Gracie, she and Johnny hoping the child would grow more independent of him before starting school. The idea seemed to be helping. But letting go of Johnny by day was different than night, and at this point they usually woke Johnny to get into bed with them. So Grace asked Gracie softly, "Do you want me to wake Johnny?"

Her pink blanket under her chin, Gracie appeared to think a moment, then shook her head. "I miss Mommy and Daddy. I can't find their stars."

Grace raised her gaze to the window, her heart hurting, too. The stars were elusive tonight, hidden by teasing wisps of clouds that slipped slowly across the sky. Her first instinct was to distract Gracie; there was so much stress in her young life—from the death of her parents to the start of school. But Gracie so rarely spoke of her pain that Grace found herself wanting to somehow comfort her. "Did you know, a long while ago, my parents went to heaven, too?"

"Are they stars?"

"I like to think so." Grace smiled wistfully. Her mother's eyes had once shone as beautifully as any star. Her father had doted on her mother, and Grace envisioned them as one endlessly glowing star.

"Are you *sad?*"

"Sometimes, just like you."

As little Gracie patted her arm, she realized the futility of trying not to get too close to this child. She sensed a bond forming that might only hurt Gracie—and her—in the end. Still, she reassured Gracie. "Mostly, I remember that they loved me and they wanted me to be happy."

The clouds parted and light from a pale quarter moon filtered through. Little Gracie leaned more heavily against her with each quiet moment. Gracie's dark lashes lowered, then lifted in her struggle to keep vigil on the sky. Finally, with a sleepy smile, she whispered, "I see Mommy's star. I see Daddy's..."

Grace held little Gracie as she slept, and knew it was too late for caution. She pressed a soft kiss to Gracie's hair. She loved this child dearly.

Johnny watched their silhouettes from his make-shift bed, listened to Grace and little Gracie's soft words fade. Grace had taken care not to let Gracie come to depend on her, but it was easy to tell that her efforts hadn't kept her from loving little Gracie. If he should lose guardianship of Gracie now—

Guilt swept over him with the darkness of a passing cloud. He hadn't intended to hurt Grace.

"Johnny? Are you awake?"

It was Grace, whispering as she leaned past little Gracie to look over the edge of the bed, probably aware of his restless stirring. Moonlight formed a corona about her, casting her in delicate silhouette. Wanting to see her better, he sat up and shifted closer to the bed.

"I'm awake."

He couldn't see the green of Grace's eyes in the darkness, but he could sense her unhappiness as if it was his own. Things had always been that way for him with Grace, Johnny realized. No matter how she tried to hide it, he'd always been able to tell when her mother was having a difficult day, if her father had had trouble at the bank again. He'd seldom failed to cheer her with his antics, though it hadn't been a conscious effort at the time. He'd simply wanted to make her smile.

This time was different. He couldn't just tease a smile out of Grace. He was responsible for her worries, her unhappiness this time. All along, he'd been aware of Grace's doubt that he could keep guardianship of Gracie. It was obvious that she needed his reassurance now more than ever.

"I was thinking about this weekend," he began. "About Gracie going to Chicago with my parents." He knew the trip to the Oceanarium troubled Grace. But while he'd intended to reassure her, voicing his parents' plan aloud somehow shook his unshakable confidence that he wouldn't lose guardianship of Gracie. He suddenly found himself at a loss for words.

Grace shifted to the edge of the bed, curling her legs beside her, tucking her nightshirt about her. He knew it was her favorite floral shirt, knew it would be slipping off her shoulder...

"Gracie's pretty excited about the trip—and seeing her grandparents."

There was no mistaking Grace's concern. But like him, Johnny knew she was grateful little Gracie was oblivious to the turmoil over guardianship. Despite the disappointments his parents had given him as a child, Johnny believed they were sincere that Gracie remain untouched by the bitter battle between them—though it was probably their lawyer's reassurance in the matter that helped sway him.

Johnny grasped at the faint resurgence of his old confidence. "It's only an overnight trip. It will be good for Gracie. After all, she has missed my folks."

"She'll miss you, too," Grace said softly, obviously attuned to his unusual lack of confidence. "You've done your best for Gracie. It's up to the court now to decide where she stays."

Grace was right, Johnny knew. He'd done everything he could do to show that he loved Gracie, that he could take care of her and raise her in the way Janelle and Grant had depended on him to do.

But what if, in spite of everything, he lost Gracie to his parents? He curled his hands in response to the gnawing fear within him. He was responsible for Gracie's happiness. And Gracie could never be as happy with his parents as she was here.

Grace rested her hand on his shoulder, and the press of her fingers was warm through his cotton T-shirt. He'd meant to reassure Grace, aware he'd brought all this upon her. Instead, she offered solace to him. Touched, he longed to take her small soft hand in his and pull her down to sit beside him. But he knew where that would lead him, so he simply accepted the comfort she offered, and silently ached for her.

They sat that way a long while in the moonlight, Johnny's desire mixed with an inexplicable yearning.

Saturday arrived all too soon. At the sound of a car's engine outside, Grace stepped out the front door onto the sunny porch, nervously brushing at her best white jeans and shirt. Earlier, she'd helped Gracie dress in new denim shorts, vest and shirt. Now she wondered where Johnny and Gracie had disappeared to after breakfast. Her attention strayed suspiciously to the garage before returning to observe Johnathan and Maureen Tremont's entrance onto the farm. Grace thought so elegant a car had never rolled down the rutted lane before.

She'd always been aware of the difference in circumstances between her family and the Tremonts. But it had never seemed to affect her relationship with Johnny and Janelle; they'd been more inclined to hang around the farm than their own home. Lately she'd come to realize how financially well-off Johnny had become in his own right. It was certainly clear he didn't have to work, if he so chose. Still, knowing Johnny could rival the Tremonts' wealth when it came to providing for Gracie gave her small measure of confidence that he could retain guardianship. The Tremonts' reputation was impeccable, their circle of friends influential.

Johnathan Tremont exited the car first. Grace had always found Johnny's parents to be somewhat intimidating and aloof. That much hadn't changed. But while Johnathan Tremont still appeared as formidably unreachable as ever at fifty, the passing years had added a tiredness to his blue eyes and silver to his hair, which had once been as dark as Johnny's. When Johnny came to stand in the open doorway of the garage, Johnathan gazed at his son, then strode wordlessly around the car to the passenger side. Johnny watched after him a long moment before calling to Gracie that her grandparents had arrived.

The lack of exchange between father and son saddened Grace. Johnathan Tremont had likely held high expectations for his only son, his namesake. He had to be proud of all Johnny had accomplished. But he hadn't been the kind to toss a ball or fish or even just talk with his son. He'd laid the groundwork for the distance between them long ago.

Johnathan offered Maureen his hand as she stepped gracefully from the car, the picture of slim elegance in trousers and silk shirt. Grace couldn't help but admire Maureen's classic dark beauty. And for a moment, her heart caught; Maureen was a lovely vision of the woman Janelle would have someday become. But Maureen didn't radiate the warmth once revealed in Janelle's shy smile. The warmth necessary to raise a happy child.

The heavy quiet that descended over the farm as they all stood assessing one another was broken by the appearance of Gracie at Johnny's side.

"Grandmother Tremont," she called. Then she hugged Johnny's leg, half hiding behind him as she peeked at her grandparents.

Gracie's shy manner, so like Janelle's, seemed to rock Maureen's cool demeanor. She paled and in that moment Grace could see her genuine grief over the loss of her daughter. Grace stepped from the porch, drawn by compassion to comfort Maureen, only to falter as Maureen composed herself, erasing all emotion from her face, save for a poised smile for Gracie.

Taking hold of Gracie's hand, Johnny led her over. Grace knew the conflict he felt with each step, heard the tension in his voice when he faced his parents and said, more for Gracie's benefit than with any regard for manners, "Hello, Mother. Father. Gracie's been looking forward to seeing the dolphins at the Oceanarium."

"We've looked forward to the trip ourselves."

Grace thought Johnathan's gravely spoken reply was enough to stifle any child's enthusiasm. But Gracie was apparently used to her grandparents' reserve, for she smiled at them, inching from behind Johnny.

"Gracie wants to show you the kittens she takes care of," Johnny went on.

"They went in the barn when it rained. Now they like it there." Gracie's little-girl voice rang in sweet contrast to the stilted adult conversation.

There was no mistaking the Tremonts' surprise over what amounted to a speech from Gracie. After a moment, Johnathan said thoughtfully, "I believe I'd like to see those kittens. Coming along, Maureen?"

Maureen hesitated enough for Grace to discern that traipsing through the barn held little appeal for the woman.

"Perhaps you'd like something cool to drink?" Grace offered. It simply wasn't in her to let Maureen disappoint Gracie.

"Johnny can carry over the kittens. And Gracie has some drawings on the refrigerator you might like to see."

"That would be fine, thank you."

Little Gracie seemed satisfied with the arrangement. She was proud of those pictures. "I can ride

Grace's bike now," she added. "I'm too big for my tricycle."

"Why don't you ride it over to the barn?" Johnny suggested, heedless as always of Gracie's attire. "We'll watch you."

Gracie ran off to the garage. The four of them watched after her, all with their own brand of pride and worry. Then Johnathan commented to Maureen, "Sounds like Gracie needs a bike for her birthday."

"That's been taken care of," Johnny said swiftly.

The moment that followed was somehow painful, marked more by strain than hostility. When Gracie pedaled out of the garage, heading for the barn, Johnny and his father walked after her, the space they left between them telling.

"He hasn't changed." Maureen's bitterness was directed unwaveringly at her son. "Johnny's just being difficult, the way he always has been."

"He's not being difficult." As Grace jumped to Johnny's defense, her nervousness vanished. "Maybe for a time he got into trouble, seeking attention, but underneath he's always been a good person. A kind person. *Always.*"

The vehemence of her words for Maureen's benefit drove them home for Grace, as well. She'd always been enamored of Johnny. But she'd only recently come to realize as she watched Johnny with little Gracie or heard him speak of her mother, exactly what it was that had drawn her to him—that drew her to him still. "He has settled down," Grace went on more calmly now, though with no less conviction. "But the best things about him, the things that make him *Johnny*—they're still the same."

"I'd like to offer you a word of advice about my son."

Something in Maureen's tone reminded Grace of a fact she'd tried not to dwell on: for the time being, she was Maureen Tremont's daughter-in-law.

"Johnathan and I are not unaware of the true purpose of your marriage with my son."

Though this was to be expected, panic stole a beat of Grace's heart. She braced herself for Maureen's threat. But Maureen only glanced toward the barn, the coolness slipping from her gaze, replaced by an unexpected look of regret. "Johnny's never had a meaningful relationship with a woman in his life," she murmured. "I would caution you, Grace, against losing your heart to my son."

Her drink forgotten, Maureen started across the yard to meet the trio coming from the barn, herding kittens. Grace stared after her, then beyond to Johnny.

Johnny lifted a kitten as he walked and held it to Gracie's cheek to tickle her. He looked vibrantly male, invincibly strong with the sun glancing off his cheekbones and dark hair, his muscled arms burnished below the black sleeves of his T-shirt. But there was a gentleness, a vulnerability about him that reached straight to Grace's heart, had it beating in a rhythm ingrained long ago.

Maureen's words of caution against losing her heart to Johnny had come years too late. Grace understood now why she'd never pursued another man to marry. She'd never stopped loving Johnny.

Only the sight of Maureen Tremont bending down to pick up a kitten was momentous enough to shake Grace out of her reverie. Johnny had once confided that he and Janelle had never had pets; his mother didn't like having so much as a goldfish around. She recalled how Johnny had taught new tricks to her dad's old farm dog, how Janelle had cried with her like a baby when it died. Grace suspected Johnny had cried, too.

And she could see that Maureen's efforts on Gracie's behalf hadn't gone unnoticed by Johnny. His expression mirrored the concern Grace felt. Like her, he was more aware than ever of his parents' determination to raise Gracie.

Johnathan was anxious to start the three-hour trip to Chicago. And when it was time to go, little Gracie's eyes grew misty, and Grace felt tears forming when Gracie tightly hugged her goodbye. Johnny had gone inside for Gracie's overnight case and now promised that her pink blanket was packed inside. He scooped Gracie up in a hug and carried her ahead to the car, where he whispered to her for a long moment. By the time his parents caught up, Gracie was climbing willingly into the car. All too quickly, they were gone, leaving only a trail of dust spiraling between the empty lane and the blue sky.

Johnny gazed stoically down the lane as the dust settled. Grace waited, wanting to comfort him, fully expecting him to head for the garage and not come out until Gracie returned. To her surprise, he turned and caught hold of her hand.

"Let's take a spin on the Harley."

He pulled her along, Grace trying to summon a reply that Johnny wasn't waiting to hear. As she followed him through the wide garage door, she grimaced at her jeans and tennis shoes, aware they wouldn't remain white for long in here.

The heavy smell of oil assailed her, rising no doubt from the black rings staining the concrete floor. There were parts everywhere, none apparently essential to the Harley's operation—at least she hoped they were not. Grace caught her lip, remembering some of Johnny's experimental repairs of the past, when her father had threatened to lock Johnny out of the garage. Maybe she should tell him "some other time."

A green helmet appeared under her nose. Not just green, but a metallic emerald she liked to think matched the color of her eyes.

"No helmet, no ride," Johnny told her as he pulled on his black helmet. He pushed on his sunglasses and climbed onto the bike, then rolled it outside to start it.

After a moment's hesitation, Grace arranged her hair behind her ears and pushed the helmet down on her head. She felt like a being from outer space, but the helmet fit perfectly. She suddenly remembered the postal delivery Johnny had received the other day. She'd assumed it was more parts; Johnny was always ordering parts. Now she wondered. This helmet looked brand-new.

Outside, Johnny revved the engine, the impatient sound at one with the look she'd seen in his eyes when he dragged her over to the garage. She hurried out, tucking back wayward strands of her hair, only to still as she caught Johnny's intent gaze upon her.

"Looks good," he said. But he looked into her eyes, not at the helmet, and a thrill shot through her.

The thrill stayed with her when she climbed onto the bike. Johnny revved the warmed engine again and she instinctively wrapped her arms around him. There was heat everywhere, from the hot sun shining down, from her body melded to his, and, as Johnny guided the bike down the lane, from the burn of the wind on her face. The bike's vibrations seemed to pulse from his body to hers until she and Johnny trembled as one. As they pulled onto the two-lane highway, gradually picking up speed, destination unknown, Grace thought she understood now why her daddy had always forbidden her to ride on the Harley with Johnny....

Late that night, windburned and weary, Grace lay awake, achingly aware of Johnny's restless stirring from across the hall in Gracie's bed. She missed Gracie. And she couldn't stop thinking about that green helmet.

Her love for Johnny had endured, had grown to encompass little Gracie. She couldn't help believing that the friendship she and Johnny had shared in the past, combined with all they had shared since he'd come back, had Johnny growing to love her in return.

Johnny shoved his hands into his jeans pockets, looking past the frosty white "G" painted on the salon window to the activity inside. He'd just left little Gracie with Grace while he went to pick up groceries for the weekend. Now he grinned, watching Gracie carefully hand pink hair rollers to Grace to wind in Mrs. Cromwell's hair. Gracie performed her task as if Mrs. Cromwell's life depended upon it, which undoubtedly, Mrs. Cromwell thought it did.

More and more, Gracie was coming out of her shell. The hurt over the loss of her parents was still deep inside her and probably would be for years to come, but he knew having Grace in her life had helped. Gracie was even looking forward to starting school on Monday with Mindy. The two girls were going to spend a night at Marcy's next week while he and Grace went to Chicago…and court.

The unease that had claimed him since his parents' successful visit with Gracie rippled through him. His lawyer had recently warned him that his parents intended to challenge the basis of his marriage to Grace quite aggressively. He gazed up the street, overcome by a need to take some sort of action to ensure Gracie's place here. The sign at the Ashville Bank suddenly beckoned.

He knew Grace was opposed to his paying the mortgage. He'd put it off, not wanting to upset her.

But it suddenly seemed imperative that this be taken care of.

He glanced back through the window, ignoring Marcy's inquisitive frown. Grace held her hands poised above Mrs. Cromwell's hair, her attention focused upon him. He saw something of the girl Grace had once been glowing in her eyes, something of the woman she'd become shining out at him. She lowered her hands, rested one upon Gracie's slight shoulder. More certain than ever that he was doing the right thing, Johnny returned her soft smile with a quick grin and headed for the bank.

In an amazingly short time, the paperwork for the payment of the Greens' mortgage was set in motion. He stopped at Gold's on his way back to the salon, leaving the store with his groceries plus two lollipops, as had become the custom with Henry. Johnny saved "his" lollipop for Gracie to share with Mindy. And he saved his news that the mortgage was paid to tell Grace at home.

Home.

Back at the farm, Johnny helped little Gracie from the truck. She ran to swing on the tire he'd hung from the elm. He leaned against the truck, looking over the farm, feeling oddly at peace considering the turmoil in his life.

He felt a tie to this land that came from something more than paying the mortgage. It came from hanging that swing for Gracie. From repairing the old truck. It came from sleeping near Grace at night, knowing little Gracie was safe in bed across the hall. It came from loving Grace.

Imagine that.

He'd seen what love *wasn't* with his parents, seen what it could be with Janelle and Grant. But one-in-a-million wasn't the best of odds. He hadn't expected to fall in love himself.

But he'd fallen in love with Grace, and his love went deep as the Greens' still pond, as though it, too, had been formed years ago.

Now he could only hope Grace was coming to realize how much he had changed, that he could be the someone special in her life.

And what better way to show her he'd changed than to attend the church social tonight?

In the summertime, the church social meant a buffet picnic in the grassy churchyard.

He'd bake a pie.

That evening, as the sky turned a dusky pink, Grace sat on a blanket, her denim dress spread over her knees as she watched little Gracie romp with a group of children while Johnny stood discussing the price of beef with Henry Gold. She thought she had never enjoyed a church social more.

He had baked a *pie*. And for the raffle, Johnny had *donated* a candle, a decorative one that the reverend won, which only seemed fitting.

He'd never once mentioned that attending would enhance their reputation as a family. He seemed to truly want to be here with her, and her belief that

Johnny's feelings for her were deepening grew stronger.

She hated to see the evening end. When they got home, she was glad when little Gracie begged to stay outside to chase fireflies in the dark.

She sat on the swing and kicked off her sandals to rock it with her bare feet, the space beside her where Janelle used to sit, empty. Johnny perched on the porch rail, the way he always had. Without words, they'd both found comfort in this arrangement since his return. But tonight, Grace wanted to change the arrangement, wished Johnny would come and sit beside her. Somehow, she didn't think Janelle would mind.

Sensing the invitation in Grace's eyes, Johnny slid from the rail and went to sit on the swing beside her. The chains chinked overhead and damp air swirled the tang of freshly mowed grass around them. He liked the comforting way their bare arms brushed, the way Grace's denim skirt crinkled against his jeans. They'd left the house lights off, and he saw the sparkle of stars in her eyes when she looked at him, the soft glow of the moon as she watched over little Gracie. Johnny sensed—hoped—that Grace felt the same need for closeness as he. The need to be a real family…

His gaze drifted to little Gracie, who was busy adding fireflies to her clear plastic jar; they'd cut air holes in the top of it and lined the bottom with grass. Johnny could remember catching fireflies for the first time in his life here on the Greens' front lawn. Three

years older than Janelle and Grace, he'd sworn them
to secrecy, insisting he was too old. But he remembered wishing he was younger, when he'd spent most
of his time back then wanting to be grown up and
on his own.

That wishful feeling came over him now. He
didn't want to be on his own anymore.

"I went to the bank today," he told Grace. It
seemed a good time to share his news, a good way
to cement the ties forming between them. "I paid the
mortgage."

Grace let the swing still, and Johnny's heart
seemed to still momentarily as well.

"You didn't have to do that."

"I told you I would. Don't you understand—I
want to do this." Couldn't she see *how much* he
wanted to?

The porch boards were cool against Grace's bare
feet, and now their dampness seemed to seep inside
her, chilling her heart, dispelling the warmth created
by Johnny's nearness. Crickets were singing, but
their resonant chirping failed to drown out Johnny's
words.

She pushed her foot against the porch floor and
said softly, "I understand."

And she did understand. Johnny's words had only
reminded her of a truth she'd foolishly forgotten: her
marriage wasn't real. Johnny didn't love her....

Chapter Nine

With a total lack of appreciation for genuine silk, Johnny tugged at the knot of his tie. The drive to the well-groomed Chicago suburb where Janelle and Grant had made their home had passed quickly enough, but it seemed he and Grace had been in this courtroom for hours. His head pounded and his stomach churned. The legal war for placement of a child was a desperate, hostile conflict that sickened Johnny, despite his determination to win.

As the prestigious Tremont family's dispute over guardianship came to a close, Johnny closed his eyes briefly, trying to dissociate himself from the proceedings, not wanting to hear a replay of the painful particulars, aware how much this battle over her child would have hurt Janelle.

He hoped Janelle's star only came out at night...

Loving people wasn't easy. He'd loved his sister

and she was gone. He loved little Gracie and feared he might lose her. He loved Grace, but he'd come to realize that losing guardianship of Gracie could mean losing Grace, as well.

She'd grown distant. Even now, as she sat close enough that her beige linen skirt draped against his dark suit trousers, Johnny sensed a reserve in her. He knew she shared the same hopes and fears as he over little Gracie. But he wasn't sure Grace had fallen in love with him, the way he'd fallen in love with her.

His lawyer indicated they should rise for the judge's final decree. Desperation overrode the sick feeling inside him. He couldn't imagine his life without Grace, any more than he could imagine having to go home to the farm and tell Gracie the "good" news, that she would get to live with her grandparents now....

His fears seemed to mesh into one giant wave that threatened to engulf him, to drag him under. His detachment crumbled, the words of the judge bringing him back to reality.

"...regarding the fitness of the child's uncle, Johnathan James Tremont, to serve as guardian..."

Johnny felt Grace tremble beside him. He caught hold of her hand to steady her, and in doing so gathered strength himself. Grace believed he'd done his best for Gracie, and he knew in his heart only Janelle and Grant could have loved Gracie more.

"...it is therefore determined the court finds no reason to overturn the testamentary guardianship of Grace Janelle Hammond..."

Yesss... With that whispered word, Johnny pulled Grace to him, burying his face in her soft silky hair until the buzz in the courtroom receded. When he pulled back, Grace's eyes shimmered with unshed tears that wet her dark lashes, and with one blink, rolled over her cheeks. Her lips curved in a tremulous smile. He held her hand, and never wanted to let go.

His lawyer pounded him heartily on the back. Jubilant, Johnny laughed, exchanging a handshake with his free hand. But the laughter caught in his throat as his gaze swept past the attorney's shoulder. He stared at his parents, struck by his mother's heartbroken expression, his father's resignation.

As Johnny let her hand slip from his grasp, Grace felt her newfound hope crushed by the uncertainty in his eyes. Even as he thanked his lawyer, he seemed to distance himself, and Grace was painfully aware Johnny's thoughts were already turning to the next step in his life.

His divorce.

Grace looked beyond the shaded porch to the daisies waving out front of the barn in the morning sunlight. As the breeze swept the long stems to and fro, the yellow petals brushed fleetingly. Grace thought how she and Johnny were like those flowers, touching only in passing these days.

The screen door opened and she turned to find little Gracie, her Snow White lunch box in hand.

"I need help with my shoe," Gracie said.

Grace crouched in her worn cutoff jeans to tie

Gracie's shoe, accustomed now to the Monday ritual of getting Gracie off to kindergarten. Most days, she drove little Gracie to school on her way to work. But on her day off, Gracie rode the school bus.

"Let's check your barrette." She adjusted Gracie's silver barrette, though there was little need to do so. They'd fussed before the mirror earlier. Still, she followed the ritual carefully, aware of the security it afforded little Gracie. Continuing the ritual, she asked, "Buttons buttoned? Snaps snapped?"

As Gracie checked her denim vest and shorts, Johnny came outside. Grace rose, moving her restless hands to the ties of the white shirt knotted at her waist. Johnny in the morning was a sight that unfailingly took her breath away—pancake flour, mussed hair and all. But this morning he was already cleaned up in jeans and his Harley T-shirt. Lately, he always had some errand to run, something to keep him busy in the garage, something to keep him away from her. That should have made things easier, but somehow it only added to the tension Grace felt of late.

"All set?" Johnny asked Gracie, ready to complete the ritual by escorting Gracie to the end of the lane to catch the bus. But little Gracie only shook her head.

"You forgot to check my lunch box," Gracie reminded Grace, sounding surprised. Grace smiled. She *always* checked Gracie's lunch box, especially if Johnny had packed it.

"That's right." She peeked in the lunch box, expecting candy. "Let's see…sandwich, apple, celery—no treat?"

Gracie patted her vest pocket. "Johnny gave me lollipops."

Of course he had. Grace looked up, lips curving.

But Johnny had moved to the top of the steps, facing down the lane. Grace turned her faltering smile on Gracie. "Sounds like you're ready to go."

She never forgot a kiss and hug, which she gave Gracie now. Obviously taking no chances, Gracie reminded her, "Don't forget my party after school."

"I could never forget that," she assured her, still overwhelmed by the prospect of ten children to entertain. She frowned. Johnny had better not avoid that.

He and Gracie started down the lane. Grace went inside, took her broom from the closet and returned to sweep the porch. Mostly she leaned on the broomstick and gazed after Johnny and little Gracie. Their journey never failed to include checking out rocks or pointing at birds in the trees. Gracie had almost missed the bus the day a toad crossed their path. Grace smiled wryly. Johnny still didn't see what all the fuss had been about. For him, skipping school had been the norm.

The bus arrived, idling to a stop, lights flashing and stop sign swung out. Once Gracie was safely aboard and headed to school, Johnny turned back down the lane. Grace swept with vigor, trying to conceal the fact that she could hardly take her eyes off him. But she was aware of every crunch of gravel beneath his shoes, aware of his tall lean body moving her way against a backdrop of blue sky. She didn't have to see Johnny's eyes to know they were the same vivid hue. But when she could see his expression clearly, she stopped sweeping, aware of the futility of her charade.

She wasn't surprised when Johnny halted in line with the garage, clearly intending to leave. The burning in his eyes that had her tugging down the short hem of her shirt was no more than the desire it appeared to be. Grace was certain Johnny only stayed at the farm now for Gracie's sake, to ensure that his parents didn't appeal the court's decision. Though she could only be happy for little Gracie, her joy was bittersweet, as it seemed destined to be since she'd first met Johnny.

Johnny pushed his hands into his jeans pockets, the restlessness that had plagued him of late evident. "I'm going to run into town, pick up some accessories for Gracie's new bike."

What else could he possibly get for the bike he'd had shipped in for Gracie's party that afternoon? Antilock brakes? An air bag? Grace let her irritation show to hide the longing inside her. Certain Johnny wouldn't come back until necessary, she said pointedly, "The birthday party starts at three-thirty."

Johnny didn't seem to notice her pique, as if in his mind he was already down the highway. Even as he spoke he was moving toward the garage. "I'll be back."

He roared out moments later on the Harley, raising dust that drifted back over her freshly swept porch.

Damn him. Grace gripped the broom handle until her hands hurt. But her frustration faded as the rumble of the Harley dwindled, leaving a lonely quiet. It wasn't Johnny's fault that she loved him. It wasn't his fault that he didn't love her.

A wistfulness came over her and she sank to the porch step, watching the daisies sway by the barn.

Johnny didn't stop until he reached the crossroad near the edge of town. Confusion poured out of him in a sweat that dampened his shirt and ran in rivulets down his temples. He thought of Grace and he ached, thought of his parents and felt the pang of regret. He didn't know what to do to appease either feeling.

Losing Gracie had seemed to age his parents the moment they'd heard the judge's decree. They'd appeared vulnerable, when he'd never seen them show their emotions before.

While he still believed little Gracie belonged here with him—and Grace—his intention wasn't to cause his parents pain. It never had been. Even back in his days of teenage rebellion, he'd wanted their approval. Their love…

Now he wanted Grace's.

He closed his eyes briefly, recalling Grace's silky hair blowing about her face this morning, her shirt revealing a strip of bare skin at her waist, her legs long and shapely below the frayed hem of her shorts.

Her green eyes, full of desire, haunted him, had him believing that maybe—

A sense of desperation swept over him. A part of him reveled in the fact that he'd fallen in love; the other part was terrified the feeling wouldn't be returned. It seemed safer to let the days pass, avoiding the prospect of divorce, hoping time worked its magic until Grace couldn't help falling in love with him.

Faced with the unlikelihood of that, with those one-in-a-million odds, Johnny turned the Harley away from town and wound it out, letting the road lead him.

Hours later, he stopped at a fork in a dusty back road. His arms vibrated with the pulse of the Harley while the sun beat down and the hot breeze flowed over him. He could almost feel Grace's arms around him, as they had been that day he'd taken her for a spin. Longing moved through him.

It was time to go home.

Dust swirling, Johnny swung the Harley in a U-turn.

With minutes to spare before little Gracie's party, Johnny rolled down the farm lane and parked before the garage. Gracie and Mindy waved to him from the front porch. From beside them, Marcy eyed him shrewdly. Grace stood impassively at the top of the steps, one hand raised to the porch rail, the breeze flirting with the skirt of her apricot flowered dress.

Johnny shed his helmet and met Grace on the porch. Gracie and Mindy ran to greet him, then returned to their task of helping Marcy set up a game of "pin the handlebars on the pink bike," Johnny's remake of the familiar "Pin the Tail on the Donkey" game. Marcy blindfolded the girls in turn, letting them practice, but Johnny was aware of the woman's watchful gaze from the far end of the porch.

Grace's silky hair swung past her sun-kissed cheeks as she gazed down at him. "I see you didn't find what you needed." Her voice was cool, but her eyes were dark.

Johnny simmered with frustration, all the more irritated because he'd forgotten the accessories for Gracie's bike. He'd been too busy thinking about Grace to remember. When Grace turned and walked into the house, he glared after her. And he pressed his hand to his heart. *Love really did hurt.*

He heard Marcy's empathetic "tsk" and glanced sharply at her.

"You poor sap," she said.

Johnny sank tiredly onto the step. As Marcy marched over in her boots, leaving the girls to play, he muttered, "What the hell's that supposed to mean?"

The hot pink flowers on her skirt offended his weary eyes, as he supposed her next words would offend his ears. To his surprise Marcy demanded, "You're in love with Grace, aren't you?"

"Maybe I am." His words laced with daring, he cocked his head, expecting Marcy's usual frown, finding sympathy instead.

"You are. It shows." She dropped down on the step beside him. "You've got kind of a 'whipped dog' look about you."

Johnny snorted at that. "How does Grace look?" he asked cautiously, fully expecting the answer to hurt him,

"She hasn't confided in me." Marcy sounded a little hurt.

"She'd have told you if she told anybody." He felt his chest squeeze. "Maybe she doesn't have anything to tell."

"There's only one way to find out."

Johnny said nothing, rather than tell Marcy he was afraid.

Naturally, he didn't have to.

"Look, much as I hate to admit it, I believe you really love Grace. I'm sorry that's not something I can tell her for you." Softening her voice she said, "Come on, you'd better get cleaned up for the party. All those little monsters will be here soon."

Johnny looked up as Marcy rose. "Thanks."

"No problem."

Mindy and Gracie chased after Marcy as she went inside, and Johnny chuckled, hearing her phony groan. Marcy's belief that he was capable of love was reassuring. He figured she recognized a changed person when she saw one.

But where Grace was concerned, it wasn't so simple. She knew the old Johnny too well. He didn't know how to make her see that he was the kind of guy who fell in love and got married. The kind of guy she'd been waiting for.

Gracie's party had Johnny putting his worries to the back of his mind for two exhausting hours. Afterward, as Marcy drove her battered Jeep down the lane with Mindy waving goodbye out the window, Johnny went into the kitchen and collapsed into a chair, loosening the collar of the dark blue shirt he'd put on after his shower.

Grace soon followed, her sandals scuffing the floor with each step. She sank into the opposite chair. Her hair was tousled, her dress wrinkled, giving her that bedroom look he found so appealing. Somehow, it stirred only tenderness in him now.

Shafts of the setting sun through the window gave the kitchen a warm antiquated glow that deepened Grace's brown hair to gold. At the front of the house, little Gracie was singing, the wheels of her pink bike crunching over patches of gravel. Johnny sensed Grace was as reluctant as he to break the peaceful spell evening had cast over them.

He could have sat there forever. But little Gracie's singing stopped and after a moment the screen door banged. Gracie's steps were heavy upon the hardwood floor as she came down the hall and into the kitchen. She crawled into Grace's lap, her small mouth turned down at the corners, and Johnny grinned knowingly. The magic of the pink bike had worn off without her friends to share it.

Grace smoothed back Gracie's sweat-dampened hair. "How about a bubble bath?"

Gracie nodded, but she only leaned back in Grace's arms.

Johnny caught Grace's worried look over little Gracie's quiet. Like him, she was probably wondering if little Gracie's thoughts were turning to Janelle and Grant as she missed them on this special day.

Instead Gracie asked, "When are Grandmother and Granddad coming? They always come for my birthday."

Grace cuddled little Gracie closer. Johnny pushed his hand through his hair, thinking of the pending arrangements between lawyers for his parents' visitation rights with Gracie. The whole situation seemed wrong.

"Grandmother always gives me a *big* present," Gracie reminded him.

Ostentatious was the word, Johnny thought. There had always been a trip, a car, or jewelry for him on his birthday. His parents just hadn't always been around to help celebrate the occasion. He wanted it to be different for Gracie. And he wanted to believe his parents felt that way, too.

"Why don't you go feed the kittens before your bath?" Johnny suggested to Gracie. "I'll see what I can do about Grandmother and Granddad."

Satisfied, Gracie went back outside. Johnny rose restlessly, as if, Grace thought, those quiet moments, the two of them sitting here, might never have been.

"This wasn't what I intended—not for Gracie or my parents," he told her, and Grace could see the pain in his eyes. "I think Mother's hurting over Gracie, and still grieving over Janelle."

Grace recalled his mother's look of regret when Maureen warned her not to fall in love with Johnny. She couldn't help thinking Maureen was hurting over Johnny, as well. "I believe you're right." She drew a fortifying breath. "Instead of waiting on the lawyer's decision, maybe you should take Gracie to see your parents."

"That's what I was thinking. For Gracie's sake, I at least have to try and make amends. I'll go give Mother a call. Tell her and Dad to expect us this weekend."

"Johnny, wait."

He paused in the kitchen doorway.

"I've…got a lot of appointments lined up Saturday. And I need to get out to the nursing home. You and Gracie go ahead and visit. Start mending those fences."

Johnny grew so somber, Grace's heart beat with encouragement. Was he disappointed? She thought she was giving him the space he so obviously needed, but maybe she was wrong....

"I'll go make plane reservations and call my parents," he finally said and left the room.

Grace sat numbly, Johnny's voice drifting to her down the hall as he left a message on his parents' answering machine saying he and Gracie would arrive in Chicago Friday night. Grace could easily envision the Tremont family coming together for little Gracie, wanted achingly to be a part of that picture.

There was a moment's quiet, then the sound of retreating footsteps down the hall. The screen door opened then closed.

Grace rested her head against her raised hands. What would she do if Johnny and Gracie didn't come back?

Chapter Ten

Despite a long day of work, Grace returned home with reluctance Saturday evening. As she stepped onto the porch, the ring of the telephone from inside quickened her pace.

Johnny.

Two rings...

Juggling her purse and a grocery sack, she crossed the porch and jiggled her key into the lock, all thumbs. She told herself to slow down. It was probably just one of her customers, or Henry Gold calling to tell her she'd forgotten a purchase. Johnny had called last night after his and Gracie's safe arrival. She didn't really expect to hear from them until they came back. If they came back...

Shaking that grim thought aside, Grace twisted the key and turned the knob. Maybe Johnny and Gracie missed her the way she was missing them.

Four rings...

Grace picked up the phone on the fifth ring, dropping her purse and settling the grocery sack on the hall table carefully so that she didn't break the lollipops Henry had sent for little Gracie. "Hello?"

"Grace? You sound out of breath."

Johnny.

"I just got home. I didn't want to miss the call if it was Gracie." *If it was you.* She forced herself to speak calmly. "Is she having a good time?"

"Yeah. Dad's taking us on a dinner cruise on the lake tonight. Here she is."

"I'm going on a boat." Little Gracie's voice chimed over the phone from the Tremonts' graystone condo in the affluent heart of the city. She sounded excited, as though she didn't miss Grace or the farm at all.

Grace reminded herself it was for the best. "That sounds like fun. You have a nice boat ride. And when you get back to your grandmother's house, have sweet dreams."

"I sleep in one of Grandmother's big beds. You could fit in it, too."

Maybe Gracie did miss her. Ever cautious of Gracie's emotional well-being, Grace said only, "That sounds like a fine enough bed for a princess. Catch my kiss now." She blew a kiss into the phone, which Gracie returned with a smacking kiss before turning over the receiver to Johnny.

"Busy day?" Johnny asked.

"Oh, yes." She'd stretched out her visit to the

nursing home to delay the lonely evening ahead. "Henry Gold sent lollipops with my groceries."

Johnny chuckled. "Good old Henry. Mother's spoiling Gracie rotten. They shopped the Magnificent Mile today. Bloomingdale's, Sak's. Nike Town."

Grace smiled wistfully. Shopping always helped draw Gracie out. "I can picture her there."

But I bet no one there had given Gracie a lollipop....

Johnny sounded so relieved things were going well with his parents, Grace couldn't help but be happy for Gracie, and for him. But her fear deepened that he and Gracie wouldn't come back.

"Tomorrow the folks are taking Gracie to the zoo. They've made a lot of plans, and I need to stop by the garage sometime and check up on business." He lowered his voice. "I also need to swing by Janelle and Grant's home to pick up some things for Gracie."

"I understand." He might be gone a while....

"I wanted to tell you we might be a while getting back. You may have to call the school Monday. Look, the folks are ready to leave. I'll be calling—"

"Goodbye, Johnny."

Chicago thrust its diamond-bright lights into the starry sky and cast them across the dark waters of Lake Michigan. Johnny moved to the rail of the cruiser he and little Gracie had boarded with his parents for dinner, the sweep of damp air across his face making him long for the Harley, a winding road and

Grace's arms wrapped around him. He and Grace hadn't had much time to talk, and he felt unsettled over their brief telephone conversation. He hadn't even told her he wished she was here. But then, Grace had sounded as if she'd been busy.

She hadn't sounded as if she was pining away for him.

His mother interrupted his worry, joining Johnny at the rail. She was perfectly groomed for the outing in her navy suit, perfectly poised save for the sadness that lingered deep in her eyes. At the time of Janelle's funeral, he hadn't been able to see the depth of his parents' pain. It somehow lessened his pain to share in theirs now.

"Gracie is having dessert with your father. She was rather insistent about lollipops."

That's my girl. Johnny grinned affectionately.

"Instead, they're having something decadently chocolate."

Because his mother sounded slightly exasperated, he reminded her, "Gracie did eat all of her vegetables."

"Your father didn't," Maureen pointed out dryly.

Johnny chuckled, looking out over the water again.

This sounded like the kind of talk he'd once heard around the Greens' kitchen table, where he and Janelle had eaten more often than not. Maybe everything was going to be okay.

"You've done well with Gracie," Maureen said, as she too gazed over the lake.

"It's been pretty easy. She likes vegetables."

"You know that's not what I mean." Maureen clasped her slender hands, diamonds flashing on her fingers. It occurred to Johnny that despite the love they'd seemed to lack as parents, love must have existed *between* his parents all these years. His resentment having burned itself out, he could only find promise in the revelation that, in their own reserved way, his parents did indeed love one another.

"In spite of everything, Gracie is happy. She's even overcoming her shyness." Maureen moved her hands restlessly. "I can't help thinking, perhaps if I'd handled things differently with Janelle—"

"When you and Dad moved us to the country, Janelle met Grace. Nothing could have helped her more."

Grace had changed his life, too—then and now. Johnny felt an ache as deep and dark as the night, missing her.

"You're right about Grace," Maureen said with quiet certainty. Her voice trembled as she went on, "But I wasn't a good mother. I can see that now. I wanted—needed—to make up for that by being a good mother to Gracie."

Understanding washed over Johnny and filled in the gulf created by his parents' attempt to take Gracie.

Maureen drew a deep breath. "I was wrong. And, in his willingness to please me, to make his own peace, your father was drawn into my wrongdoing. Grace will be a much better mother to Gracie than I've ever known how to be."

Johnny looked at his mother then. His parents had openly challenged his marriage in court; now he desperately hoped his mother saw something in his marriage that he couldn't.

"She's grown up to be quite a woman." Maureen covered her son's hand on the rail, felt a mother's pride, however undeserved, over the man he had become. A man whom she had seen Grace Green loved whole-heartedly. She hoped her words would help Johnny to recognize that love.

But she would not interfere.

"I want only to be a good grandmother to Gracie." Her voice wavered. "I want to be a good mother to my son."

Johnny turned up his palm and held his mother's hand tightly. "I think you're doing just fine."

Maureen's tremulous smile turned wry as a family of six made their boisterous way to the rail nearby. "Tourists. Do you know your father declined an invitation to the opera to take this cruise?" Maureen watched the children a moment longer. "I believe I'll go join him and Gracie."

As his mother walked off, Johnny curved his lips in a contemplative smile. He didn't expect her to change who she was. Amazingly, she hadn't asked that of him either. But they were both trying.

He turned back to the rail. He could envision little Gracie's future more clearly now, and that calmed him—somewhat. She was going to be quite the little lady someday, as much at home shopping the elegant length of Michigan Avenue as she was skipping the quaint Main Street of Ashville. She would be raised in the best of both worlds, raised with love.

But they needed Grace to make that love whole.

A feeling of desperation came over him. Making amends with his parents left him no reason to stay married to Grace—unless she loved him.

Across the water, the skyline glittered with all the decorativeness of Christmas. But it was the stars overhead Johnny sought as he prayed Grace was missing him, too.

Grace turned on the old Victrola she'd carted out of the attic. Elvis's crooning voice filled the living room for the umpteenth time that evening. She closed her eyes briefly. Maybe it hurt, but she couldn't help that she'd fallen in love with Johnny all those years ago.

She sighed. She needed one of Marcy's whiskey-and-honeys to comfort her out of her melancholy.

She needed Johnny.

Filmy curtains billowed at the window, teasing at her skin below the sleeves of her nightshirt. Grace peered into the darkness outside. She half expected to find a storm brewing. There were clouds, but the breeze was cool and dry and persistent, drawing her out onto the porch.

She rested her hands on the porch rail, her night-shirt whipping against her as a strong gust blew, chilling her legs and bare feet. Music played softly from behind her, while before her, the whistle and rush of the wind through the trees seemed lonely.

She was lonely.

She missed Johnny and little Gracie. And tonight, more than ever, she missed Janelle. Her confidante. Only Janelle would understand how much she was hurting now over Johnny.

The limbs of the elm swayed heavily, their shadows waltzing over the porch floor in time to the music. Shadows cast by a moon hung in a clearing sky filled with stars.

Janelle...

"I still love him," Grace whispered. "I'll always love Johnny and little Gracie."

The stars seemed to listen, to wink and nod at her through the darkness.

Soothed, Grace made her way back into the house.

Outside the wind calmed, the daisies by the barn growing still, their soft petals touching.

"Don't forget to bring my toys."

Gracie came on the run in her new tennis shoes to where Johnny waited in the foyer to hug her goodbye. He was on his way to Janelle's suburban home, while Gracie was waiting to leave for the zoo with his parents. He leaned down and she wrapped her small arms about his neck, her fingers curling into his T-shirt as he lifted her in a hug. "I won't forget," he promised.

Gracie hadn't wanted to go with him, and Johnny liked to think it was because she was healing, moving on with her young life.

"Bring my video games. And all of my dolls. And

my farm book with the kittens in it,'' Gracie instructed.

''Video games. All of your dolls. Farm book with kittens. Got it.'' Settling Gracie on her feet, he chuckled, thinking it might be easier just to bring every box marked ''toys.''

''When are we going home, Johnny?''

Johnny hesitated, in the process of pulling the keys to his parents' BMW from his jeans pocket.

Home...

''You mean back to the farm?'' Wasn't that what he'd intended? To make Ashville home? So why did he suddenly suspect Gracie's meaning had become more specific?

Gracie nodded. ''Am I going to *skip school?*''

Naturally, she'd overheard his comment to Grace. Despite the fresh worry that gripped him, he had to smile. ''Only if you have to.'' He knelt before little Gracie. ''I guess you miss those kittens. That's why you want your farm book.''

''I want Grace to read it to me.''

''I guess...you miss Grace, too.''

Gracie nodded vigorously. ''I'm going to give her a *big* kiss when I see her.''

''She'll like that.''

''I know.''

Of course Gracie knew. Children knew when they were wanted and loved, just as they knew when they weren't.

''I have to go eat my pancake now.''

"Tell your Grandmother and Granddad that I'm leaving."

Gracie ran off. Johnny rose, feeling as if each time one weight rolled off his chest, it was replaced by another. As careful as Grace had been, little Gracie had grown to love her.

The thought plagued him on the drive to the suburbs.

He parked the car in the sweeping driveway and got out. The fifteen-room condo where his parents resided was impressive; Janelle and Grant's modern two-story mansion was no less so.

But as the massive front door opened and shut with a silent swing, Johnny thought it lacked character in comparison to the banging screen door at the farmhouse. Stained glass windows on either side of the entrance let in soft light that glanced off delicate, pale walls that would have benefited, in Johnny's opinion, from a few of the Greens' old Elvis prints. The pool beyond the veranda had been drained, but even at its clear-blue best it couldn't compare with the farm's moss-covered pond on a hot sunny day. Johnny wondered if Grace might be fishing now....

He walked toward the stairs, dust covers and boxes failing to diminish the home's elegance. His apartment had sported many of the amenities this immense house offered. A Jacuzzi. A fireplace. Skylights. He'd never missed either place when he'd taken Gracie to Ashville. But he missed the Greens' old farm and knew it was because he'd left a part of himself there. His heart.

Now he knew the same could be said for little Gracie.

Ascending a hardwood staircase suitable for filming *Gone With The Wind,* Johnny slid his hand up the banister. At the top, Johnny caught the star-like glint of sun upon silver through an open doorway. Janelle and Grant's room.

Though he was here to gather things for Gracie, Johnny didn't turn toward her dollhouse of a room. He went into Janelle's room, drawn to a box of lace finery that spilled onto the floor, candlesticks and other silvery knickknacks crushing down the lace in the center of the box. It occurred to him that his sister had been a romantic. The stained glass, the stairway, the lace, the candlesticks.

Johnny knelt by the box, rubbing his thumb over traces of tarnish on Janelle's silver jewelry chest. He should have packed these things more carefully—just as he should have been more careful with little Gracie's heart…and Grace's.

He hoped—prayed—this separation from Grace would have her realizing that she loved him. But if that wasn't the case—and it didn't seem to be so— he wasn't the only one who would be hurt. And more hurt was the last thing little Gracie needed. The silver blurred beneath his touch. He hadn't meant to let Janelle down.

The jewel chest sprang open beneath his hand, letters unfolding accordion-like from inside. He blinked, clearing his vision as he pushed the papers back inside. Fine ivory paper. Johnny slid his thumb across engraved double "G's." This was the stationery Janelle had given Grace for her fifteenth birthday.

Letters from Grace...

Johnny lifted a letter from the box. It wasn't postmarked, and he realized she and Janelle must have traded notes that same summer, after he'd left Ashville.

His conscience overriding his curiosity, Johnny tried to put back the letter, but the sticky corner where it folded into an envelope for mailing stuck to his thumb.

Maybe it was a sign.

Johnny read the letter.

Dear Janelle,

I am in my room and it is dark outside. Dad has just helped Mama to bed. Sometimes, she doesn't know him, and he pretends it doesn't matter, but I can tell his heart is broken.

My heart is also broken now that Johnny is gone. I know you are sad, too. I think the whole town misses him, even though most said he was trouble. Deep down, they know that Johnny is special.

Keep your promise never to tell him I love him. I want him to stay my friend, in case he ever comes back.

Dad is playing Elvis on the phonograph. Elvis is singing *Can't Help Falling In Love*. I hope it won't always hurt this much.

Love, Grace.

Johnny sat in silence. Stunned. Disbelieving. Shallow breaths passed his lips.

She'd loved him. Grace Green had loved him when he was Ashville's bad boy. She'd loved him when he'd lived to tease her, loved him even when he'd unknowingly broken her heart.

Special.

If Grace had thought he was special back then, he must qualify for a Nobel now. But he couldn't help wondering, hoping, praying that if she'd loved him for who he was then, she might love him now. He might be that one special love in her life.

He gently closed the jewelry chest, let the stars of light shine upon it. "Thanks, Janelle," he whispered.

Johnny let the Greens' old truck roll into the curb as he parked before the salon. An exact reenactment of his first day back in Ashville required the Harley, but he'd thought that might push his luck in the wrong direction. He'd planned a few subtle changes anyway. He opened his door and lifted a smiling little Gracie out of the truck.

At the sound of the truck door closing, Grace set down her watering can near a potted plant. Through the salon window the sight of the old green pickup, Johnny standing on the sidewalk beside it, sent her heart into a cautious, hopeful beat. Johnny looked lean and handsome in jeans and a white T-shirt. Little Gracie, dressed in her pink denim, was adorable at his side. Sunbeams formed distinct halos about their dark hair.

Grace straightened her denim jumper with shaky hands, smoothing the snug white T-shirt beneath it. She fluffed her bangs and ran her fingers through the length of her hair. She walked to the door and opened it, bracing her hand on the frame.

"Perfect." Johnny pulled off dark glasses and Grace caught the gleam in his blue eyes. The smile he flashed sent the hesitant beat of her heart into overdrive. "Gracie needs a haircut."

Then Johnny's smile softened, faded to that solemnness that never failed to touch her.

"Gracie needs *you*. And so do I."

Don't let him be teasing. Let this be real, Grace prayed.

"I don't know…it's Monday and the salon is closed." Grace winked at little Gracie, as if her whole future didn't revolve around Johnny's next move.

He leaned down and whispered to little Gracie. Gracie ran over and Grace was caught up in a hug and a kiss that somehow reassured her, yet made her all the more uncertain.

Gracie skipped inside, climbing into Grace's chair at her styling station. Grace trembled at Johnny's approach, old hurt lurking at the brink of her heart, threatening to spill over with new.

"I do need you, Grace. And not just for Gracie's sake. I love you. And I know now that you loved me years ago. I believe you could love me again, if you'll just give me a chance to convince you.''

He knew... There had been a time when she would have died rather than have Johnny Tremont realize she was in love with him. Now his eyes seemed to have absorbed all the pain and longing she'd once carried in her heart. Could she really be the one who could chase that hurt from his eyes?

''I'm not that different from the girl I used to be,'' Grace warned him.

''You were my *friend*.'' Johnny's smile was slow and sure. ''I couldn't help falling in love.''

It seemed to be all she needed to hear. ''I've never stopped loving you, Johnny. Don't ever change, and I'll love you forever.''

Johnny pulled her into his arms, burying his face in the curve of her neck. Grace breathed in the masculine, motor-oil scent of him, relished the strength of him as he held her. But it was his shuddering breath against her skin, revealing the gentleness within him, that melted her heart.

She leaned back to look at him. ''How did you know that I loved you all those years ago?''

''Tonight, after Gracie's asleep, we'll go look at the stars and I'll tell you.''

Grace smiled then. *Janelle*. ''We'll take good care of Gracie. We'll make sure she knows how much Janelle and Grant loved her. And how much we love her, too.''

Johnny gave her a look so warm, it stirred a fire within her. ''I want to give Gracie a brother or sister.

And if you want, I'll buy you the biggest diamond they have on Michigan Avenue.''

''A brother or sister for Gracie sounds perfect. But I don't want another ring. I want a honeymoon.''

Johnny's eyes darkened. ''I'll take you anywhere.''

Grace considered, then glanced up at him from beneath her lashes. ''Why don't you *take me*...on the Harley.''

And Grace drew Johnny down for a kiss that smothered his laughter.

From inside on her chair, little Gracie heard them laugh, watched Grace kiss Johnny on his lips. And while that wasn't how it happened in the book, she decided it was better than when the Prince kissed Snow White.

*   *   *   *   *

ATTENTION ALL
SANDRA STEFFEN
FANS!

Silhouette Books proudly presents four
brand-new titles by award-winning author
Sandra Steffen for your reading pleasure.

Look for these upcoming titles in 1998:

In February
MARRIAGE BY CONTRACT (*36 Hours* Book #8)
Sandra Steffen's contribution to Silhouette's latest
continuity series is a marriage-of-convenience story you
won't forget.

In April
NICK'S LONG-AWAITED HONEYMOON
(SR#1290, 4/98)
The popular *Bachelor Gulch* series continues with a tale
of reunited lovers.

In July
THE BOUNTY HUNTER'S BRIDE (SR#1306, 7/98)
This contribution to Silhouette's newest promotion,
Virgin Brides, is a story of a shotgun marriage that leads
to the most romantic kind of love.

And coming your way in December from
Silhouette Romance, *Bachelor Gulch's* most famous
bachelorette, Louetta, finally gets the man of her dreams!

Don't miss any of these delightful stories…
Only from Silhouette Books.

Available at your favorite retail outlet.

▼ *Silhouette*®

MATERNITY LEAVE

Coming September 1998

Three delightful stories about the blessings
and surprises of "Labor" Day.

TABLOID BABY by Candace Camp

She was whisked to the hospital in the nick of time....

THE NINE-MONTH KNIGHT
by Cait London

A down-on-her-luck secretary is experiencing
odd little midnight cravings....

THE PATERNITY TEST by Sherryl Woods

The stick turned blue before her
biological clock struck twelve....

*These three special women are very pregnant...and very
single, although they won't be either for too much longer,
because baby—and Daddy—are on their way!*

Available at your favorite retail outlet.

The World's Most Eligible Bachelors are about to be named! And Silhouette Books brings them to you in an all-new, original series....

World's Most Eligible Bachelors

Twelve of the sexiest, most sought-after men share every intimate detail of their lives in twelve never-before-published novels by the genre's top authors.

Don't miss these unforgettable stories by:

Dixie Browning

MARIE FERRARELLA

Jackie Merritt

Tracy Sinclair

BJ James

RACHEL LEE

Suzanne Carey

Gina Wilkins

VICTORIA PADE

MAGGIE SHAYNE

Anne McAllister

Susan Mallery

Look for one new book each month in the
World's Most Eligible Bachelors series beginning
September 1998 from Silhouette Books.

Silhouette®

Available at your favorite retail outlet.

International bestselling author

JOAN JOHNSTON

**continues her wildly popular Hawk's Way
miniseries with an all-new, longer-length novel**

THE SUBSTITUTE GROOM

HAWK'S WAY

August 1998

Jennifer Wright's hopes and dreams had rested on her summer wedding—until a single moment changed everything. Including the *groom*. Suddenly Jennifer agreed to marry her fiancé's best friend, a darkly handsome Texan she needed—and desperately wanted—almost against her will. But U.S. Air Force Major Colt Whitelaw had sacrificed too much to settle for a marriage of convenience, and that made hiding her passion all the more difficult. And hiding her biggest secret downright impossible...

**"Joan Johnston does contemporary Westerns
to perfection."** —*Publishers Weekly*

Available in August 1998
wherever Silhouette books are sold.

PSHWKWAY